T4-AKA-163

Absolutly
spell binding
fast paced
A Excitment near

CANDLELIGHT REGENCY

murders spys
good stuff +10

CANDLELIGHT ROMANCES

FRIARY'S DOR

✣✜✜✜✜✜✜✜✜✜✜✣

Betty Hale Hyatt

A CANDLELIGHT REGENCY

For Lucinda and Lynne

Published by
Dell Publishing Co., Inc.
New York, New York 10017
Copyright © 1973 by Betty Hale Hyatt

specifically for inclusion in a magazine or newspaper.
Dell ® TM 681510, Dell Publishing Co., Inc.
Printed in the United States of America
First printing—January 1973

FRIARY'S
DOR

CHAPTER ONE

LONG white streamers of mist trailed inward from the Channel and groped across the low-lying fields and orchards by the time I reached the dip in the chalk cliffs where they came down to meet the sea, forming the small irregularly shaped cove. The late November sun flamed suddenly in the west, turning the sky to dark crimson as it perched just above the bank of fog before dropping into it.

I glanced at the now gray-green surface of Friars Cove and caught my breath in surprise; a few yards from where I stood was a small quay, a boat tied alongside. Out farther lay a ship at anchor, her high poop deck riding on the gentle swell, the name *The Dark Lady* painted in gold on the stern.

There was no one about, and the silence was broken only by the lap of the water. Shrouded as it was by the fog so hidden from the open Channel, and the ship could have easily been a phantom.

A strange spasm of fear and excitement raced down my spine as I thought this could easily be one of the many smuggler vessels that were known to rampage this isolated coastline. Why not? The nearly abandoned cove was perfect. My hands felt clammy. Where was Tom Pegnally? Surely he looked after the place well enough since my Grandfather Lawrence had died. And Jason, too. No smugglers would use Friars Cove openly without their knowledge.

I turned and hurried up the path, making my way around the old tower and across the springy turf to the cloisters, glancing around furtively as I did so. There would be no welcome tonight, no warm fire and no food except what I had with me, for none of the servants knew I was coming.

The front door to the house was locked, and the only place I knew would be open was the old friars' infirmary where my grandfather had treated his patients and where he taught me all he could about his profession of doctoring the sick. I went through the cloisters, barely glancing at the dark house closed tight against intruders, and crossed a small cobblestone courtyard to the back of the house and to the infirmary adjacent to the kitchen gardens and the servants' hall in the house.

The door was heavy oak, nail-studded, and it opened to my touch. I was inside when I realized the truth, and before I could move, the door slammed shut. I was seized from behind by a hand that gripped my arm, jerking me around bodily.

Never had I been so startled; fear clutched my heart when I looked up into the face of the man who held me. Indeed, his fingers pressed painfully into my flesh under the velvet pelisse I wore.

The light from the fire in the fireplace flickered over a face burned bronze by sea winds or tropical suns, but it was the eyes that startled me most. They were brilliant dark eyes, inscrutable, under magnificent black brows.

In that brief moment, our eyes met and held; his

seemed to penetrate mine. Something odd stirred inside me, an elation quite unfamiliar in spite of the fear. He was the most handsome man I'd ever seen in my life.

"What are you doing here?" he demanded, his voice strong and deep, used to being obeyed, I thought. He was standing quite close to me—too close, and he still gripped my arm tightly.

It took all the nerve I could muster to answer him. "I might ask that of you, my lord," I said, staring at him defiantly.

He stepped back a pace to regard me, narrowing those dark eyes, and as he did so, he grimaced. He was tall, somewhere in his late twenties, I guessed, and rather swashbuckling in the black skirted coat and buckskin breeches above the Hessian boots.

It was then I saw the cause of that grimace. Blood was oozing through a torn hole in the sleeve of his right arm below the shoulder.

"You're hurt," I said calmly, lowering my gaze to the wound.

He stared at me hard, searching my face; then his eyes traveled over my pelisse and gray bonnet. "What are you doing in this house, madam! Answer me!" He stood in front of me, not moving, with a kind of lounging grace in spite of his bleeding arm.

I held my head up, determined not to let him frighten me. "Very well," I said testily. "Since you demand it, my lord, this is my house, and I've just returned home. I might ask why you're here, but truly, my good sir, you're bleeding quite badly, you know. That arm should be treated, and now. Please allow me to help you. I do know my business, you see. I'm a nurse."

He studied me for a long moment, then he seemed

to relax. "I have a musket ball in my arm. Can you cut it out?"

"I can try," I said, looking steadily up at him, our eyes measuring each other. He nodded and I glanced around the room.

It was one of two, the other being a small ward of sorts with a few beds. This room had a wide fireplace with a fire glowing and a kettle of water already heating next to the large copper cauldron at one end; there were some cabinets whose shelves were filled with the jars and bottles my grandfather had stored there, with labels on them to denote their contents.

In a glance I saw what already had been in preparation; it was evident that he had planned to remove the ball himself. I glanced up at him; he was watching my face.

"Take off your coat and shirt. I'll get the bandages and the instruments ready. There are two candles in that drawer over there. We'll need some light. And please sit down there at the table." I indicated the table in the center of the room to which two chairs and a bench had been drawn up.

I took off my pelisse and bonnet and hung them on the wooden peg behind the door. As I turned, I saw the man still watching me, and I guessed him to be as puzzled about my presence as I was about his.

"Here," I said, going over to him. "Let me help you with your coat. How long ago did this happen?" He allowed me to help him, and as I took the coat, I noticed the pair of cavalry pistols he wore. These he took off as I hung the coat beside mine. The material was fine, and I guessed that he was a gentleman, no doubt a titled one from the looks of his clothing.

"Not over an hour, I should say. It was an accident—

a hunting accident," he said casually. While he lit the two candles, I covered my blue muslin gown with a white apron I fished out of a cupboard, along with a bottle of cognac and some Scotch that had been stored exactly where Grandfather had placed it. Alongside these I placed a pewter cup. Then I found a basin and poured the hot water in it, washing my hands first. As I prepared the small sharp instrument and bandages I had taken from the cabinet, I could feel the man's eyes on me.

He had unbuttoned his shirt and had started to remove it, but I saw he was having difficulty, so I began to help. When I touched his arm, I was suddenly aware of his nearness. Never in my life had I seen a man bare to his waist, and certainly I had never been alone with one like this. I folded his shirt and placed it on the bench.

His shoulders were broad, muscular, and tanned; his skin was warm to my touch as I gently soaked the wound where the blood had begun to clot.

I said: "You may have a drink, sir, before I start. It will help relieve the pain."

"I don't need it—not now, at least."

While I poured some fresh hot water into the basin, I glanced at him. What was he doing here, anyway? Surely, he couldn't have known about the infirmary unless he was familiar with it, which apparently he was, I thought, as he placed the candles close by.

He sat down and put his elbow on the table, to steady it, while I began probing the torn flesh with my fingers. He helped me by holding the flesh with his fingers, our heads close together.

"There it is," he said, and while he held it, I quickly but gently removed the half-inch ball and placed it

down on a strip of gauze. "You're lucky it didn't tear
into a muscle tendon," I said as I cleaned the wound.
While he was watching, I poured some of the pure
alcohol into it. Then I quickly sewed the flesh together
in three neat stitches.

"It will hurt now, but the alcohol will prevent infec-
tion later on," I said softly, carefully bandaging it with
fresh muslin.

"I think I'll have that drink now," he said. I poured
some cognac into the pewter cup and gave it to him.
As he took it, our eyes met above the rim of the cup.
"Thank you. You're very good, you know. Skilled, I
mean. Where did you learn to do this?"

His glance took in my gown of fine Indian muslin,
now threadbare, which I hoped he hadn't seen in the
dim light.

"My Grandfather Lawrence taught me," I said as I
began to clean away the surgery. "He was Doctor Lawrence here at Friary's Dor for almost forty years. In
fact, he was the village doctor."

"Was? Isn't he now?"

"No. He's dead."

"Oh. I'm sorry."

"Don't be. It was a long time ago. Three years, in
fact."

He was drinking thoughtfully from the cup. Then he
asked, "Have you been away? I understood you to say
you've just returned. I wasn't aware the house was oc-
cupied—" He stopped, lifting those magnificent dark
brows in question.

"Or you wouldn't have trespassed?" I said lightly,
lifting my own brows. "But of course you're right. I
did say I've just returned. I intend to stay here now,
too. It's mine, you see. My grandfather left it to me."

He swallowed a sip of his drink, watching me as I took a tin down from one of the shelves and measured some Indian tea into an earthen pot, then poured hot water over it to let it steep.

"Where have you been?" His voice was pleasant.

I paused, looking at him for a moment, then went to fetch the little wicker basket I'd carried with me and brought out the steak and kidney pie I had purchased at the inn in Canterbury where the coaches had changed. I broke it in two pieces and placed them on a pewter plate on the table.

Of course, I couldn't tell him the truth—I wouldn't—only part of it. "I've just been through one of the most devastating seasons a woman can ever go through," I said gently, smiling, and sitting down across the table from him. "I've been put through the 'coming out' in London's best society, but it didn't pay off, and here I am back at Friary's Dor without a suitable husband, in hiding for now and for what it's worth, and knowing my father will most likely find me here and try to change my whole life by bartering me in some gruesome arrangement if he can!"

There was a glimmer of secret laughter in his eyes as he said: "You sound bitter, but determined. Can't you refuse?"

"That is precisely why I've come home, to build up enough courage to face Father and tell him nothing will change my mind. Maybe he won't remember Friary's Dor for a while, I hope."

"Why would your father want you to marry against your will unless it is for gain?"

"For gain?" I almost laughed. "Oh, it is not for gain, sir, that my father wants me married off. It's for the sole purpose of getting me off his hands. I'm a burden, you see—a responsibility, ever since my mother died, and his military mind cannot cope with me. After my grandfather's death, he sent me to London to see me 'properly out' by one of London's famous hostesses, the Lady Deveril, so that I could meet a suitable match—a husband, if you please, but no offers came my way. And so Lady Deveril wrote my father and told him my case was hopeless. So now Father plans to do it himself."

I didn't mention the secret life I had been involved in, or that it had backfired and I was almost caught; indeed, I was certain that French diplomat had recognized my face. That was the reason I had to leave London.

"What does your father plan?" he asked, watching as I poured the tea into the cups and offered it to him with some of the pie. He took it gratefully, with a nod of his head.

"To get me married."

He glanced into the firelight, and I noticed that secret laughter around his mouth again. "I gather from all this that you ran away."

"I did." I took a bite of the pie and found it delicious. He ate, too, and I was glad to see that he enjoyed it.

"You were brave to do that, were you not? I'd say you have more than enough courage to meet your father."

"You don't know my father. He is Sir Reginald Dillard, one of Sir Arthur Wellesley's officers in the 52nd Regiment."

"I believe they are in Portugal, not in England," he said.

"Father informed me by letter that he was taking a

leave and would see to my future arrangements during that time. I simply left Lady Deveril's gracious house in St. Johns Wood and came here. Father will be angry."

"I see," he said, taking another bite of the pie. "What arrangements has he made? Do you know if he has someone in mind?"

I stared at him; we were in a most cozy room, and I was bolder than my experience had warranted me to be, talking in this nature to a perfectly strange man. The firelight flickered around us, creating a sudden intimacy. But I didn't care. I liked him for his interest.

"I really don't know, nor care, since it is not going to affect me," I said softly. "I simply won't have it. I won't be bartered like that and, anyway, I have no dowry to speak of. He can't make me marry."

"What do you plan to do, then, if you refuse his—arrangement?"

"I plan to live right here at Friary's Dor. I'll take care of the sick, just like my grandfather taught me. The farms, small though they are, will be ample, and then there's the winery. Tom Pegnally truly makes the best cider in these parts, if I may brag. I won't be idle. And I won't give it up for marriage with someone I don't even know!" Without knowing why, tears welled up in my eyes, and I averted my gaze from his, brushing away the wetness with the back of my hand.

"I'm sure you have nothing to worry about," he said with sudden tenderness. "No, you mustn't cry about it." He stood up and came around to stand beside me. He took my hand and pulled me to my feet, then cupped my chin in one hand. I forgot everything except that his eyes were looking into mine.

There was no time to think, no time to remember

who we were, save the desire and need that was intense; it pulsed between us, strong and vibrant. He pulled me to him, his warm mouth seeking mine, and we clung together.

How long we stood there, I don't know. Trembling all at once, I tried to draw away. "My lord," I said, but my voice broke, and our eyes held. My breath quivered, and he pulled me to him again, his kisses more demanding, scorching my skin as a fire raced along my blood stream.

All at once a groan escaped him, and he stepped away from me unexpectedly. I feared I had hurt his arm, but he turned and picked up his shirt from the bench where I had placed it earlier. He walked over to the fireplace, his back to me for a moment, staring down at the flames. A burning log snapped, the only sound in the room. Then he turned to me.

"You must believe that I had no intention for this to happen, Miss Dillard," he said almost angrily. "Please try and put it from your mind. It should not have happened, and it won't again." His voice was rough, and something in that lean brown face closed up as he began to put on his shirt.

Stricken, I could only stare, knowing a terrible sense of shame wash over me. I was wanton—no lady would have allowed this to happen at any cost. I lowered my eyes. "It was . . . not your f—ff-ault, sir," I said, my voice low. My cheeks were flaming scarlet, and I bit my lip to hold the tears back while turning my back to him.

A few minutes of silence passed. "Don't blame yourself," he said in gentler tones, and came over to me. As I looked up, his eyes were measuring me.

"You have been most gracious, my lady, and I'm truly in your debt. You probably have saved my arm, not to mention my very life, perhaps." His words were gentle but cool, I thought.

He strode to the door, then hesitated and turned again to me, fastening the gun belt around his waist. I took his coat down and helped him into it. Then he placed his hands on my shoulders.

"Please do me one more favor, Miss Dillard. Don't take in strangers as you have this night. You may be . . . ravaged. This comes as a friendly warning. Do be more careful in the future."

Then he was gone.

For a moment my thoughts were too chaotic to feel anything. Then, as the realization struck me that he was indeed gone, I began to tremble. I had been most indiscreet; no lady would have entertained even a thought about the behavior I had allowed from this man—a perfect stranger. He told me as much.

He hadn't talked of himself but had pried all my grievances out into the open. And I had allowed him to. Why hadn't he "ravaged" me?

Why had he been shot? And how did he find his way to Friary's Dor, to the infirmary, no less, to seek refuge? Unless he knew about it and was familiar with it. Why hadn't Tom Pegnally's hounds given the alarm—unless the man were known?

Suddenly I knew that the man did know more about Friary's Dor than he let on. He must have been from that ship anchored in the cove. But of course!

I understood then that it had been no hunting accident that sent a musket ball into his arm. It had to be someone pursuing him—a revenue agent, perhaps?

All of a sudden I went weak in the knees; I sat down, staring into the flames, frightened now as I'd not been before.

Suppose I had been followed here; Anthony had warned me to be careful, that strange things happened to British agents who were caught by the enemy. They had a way of disappearing, he'd said. And now I had entertained and aided a possible smuggler or even a secret agent for the French!

CHAPTER TWO

As if in a daze, I stood up and cleaned the room, putting away the instruments and bandages; I washed the teapot and cups, wiped the crumbs off the table, and afterward sat down in front of the fire again, my thoughts in a turmoil.

I would liked to have put the whole encounter from my mind, but this I could not do. How easily I could have been possessed by that man! The thought made me tremble, remembering the boldness of those dark eyes and the way he had held me in his arms.

Not once had I ever felt like that with Anthony; Captain Anthony Cordell, of the Light Dragoons, daring, dashing, terribly handsome, and always getting me involved in those international intrigues that were a part of his life in London and abroad.

My thoughts went back to those months I had agreed to help him. At first it had proved to be exciting, so vastly different from the otherwise boring life I was leading.

"You can help me more than you suspect, Honor," Anthony had said one evening shortly after we had met at Lady Deveril's house. "Since you speak foreign languages so well, the information of Napoleon's plans which Sir Percival wants and needs can be easily gained. All you have to do is listen. Their wives talk among themselves. You can simply listen in innocence, and no one will suspect you understand them."

Sir Percival was one of the heads of British Intelligence, and Anthony once told me Sir Percival was a relation. "It's because of this that I now have this position with the Home Office myself. Please say you'll help me, Honor."

I had agreed all too readily, I believed now. It had become dangerous and I knew, without a doubt, that I had been found out. Why else had I been followed that night? And later, while I was preparing for bed, had someone come into my room? I had seized the chance to slip out through a French window and hide myself in a maid's room, terrified the rest of the night. For two days I had been frozen with terror, and then my chance came to leave. It had been my only alternative in the end.

Now I glanced around me in the warmth of this room, still knowing a sense of that same terror, and then returned my gaze to the flames. So engrossed was I in my thoughts that I didn't hear the voices and footsteps until they were outside the door. I jumped up, my heart fluttering oddly.

The door burst open, and there stood Grace and her husband of three years, Jason Dare. Grace, my old nanny, though she wasn't old, had brought me home from Calcutta, India, when I was seven, the year my mother had died, and she had been with me until Grandfather's death when I went to London. I knew she now lived with Jason in the carriage house.

Round and firm, Grace's cheerful face registered shock: "My dear life, but what on earth are you doing here in this old place, Honor? What a scare you gave

us, coming down here alone like this and not letting
me know? The minute Jason brought in your trunks
and boxes, I knew you'd done something foolish, like
walking all the way from Three Friars Inn! Are you all
right, child?" Her small gray eyes stared at me with in-
tensity.

"Of course I'm all right, Grace," I said, astonished.
"But what—How on earth did you know I was here?"

Jason, not much taller than Grace and rather portly,
dressed warmly in his brown great coat, grinned affably and said: "Why miss. I was in the village after
the stagecoach came in, and the driver said to see that
your baggage got to Friary's Dor. I was late getting in,
but Mrs. Dare was sure you'd be up to the house by
now. But it were locked, and Dust and Mrs. Barrows
had to come along to unlock it, but you bain't there."

"We thought to come in here, Honor, as I knew
you'd know it was open. It was the most likely place,
remembering that you always used to come in here."
Grace reminded me of a little gray sparrow with her
gray cloak and bonnet, her voice rather chirping-like.
"And I recalled how well you always liked to walk
along the chalk cliffs, and we simply guessed you'd be
in here. And to think that you came to this cold, old
dark house without a word you were coming! You
might've caught your death, not to mention running
into them smugglers!"

"Smugglers?" I asked, my heart pounding loudly
against my ribs. "What smugglers?" I saw the look pass
between Jason and Grace.

"Now miss," Jason said heartily. "Mrs. Dare don't
aim to scare ye none with that kind o' talk. But to be
on the safe side, it do be best if ye don't go walking
about on this coast these days, lonely that it be. But

things have been happening, and it bain't safe fer a lady like ye to be here and alone." His small black eyes almost snapped in the firelight as he glanced around him in the room.

Thank God I had the sense to clean up all traces of the hour just past, I thought. It wouldn't do to have servants know of that encounter, not even Grace.

"No, it isn't safe for you to be alone, Honor," Grace said. She had never called me 'miss' as the other household servants did because she had been like a mother to me. "Why didn't you come down to the carriage house, love, instead of here?" She glanced around her, then back to me, as Jason went to the door and "halooed" loudly to the house.

"I was going to in the morning. But tonight I simply wanted to be alone. I've come back, Grace. To stay for good. The house will have to be opened, and we might as well get started on the cleaning. Father will be coming," I said with a grimace of annoyance, "so it's just as well to get it over with. I plan to stay in here tonight—"

"Not on my life you don't!" Grace was aghast. "T'is not fit for a peasant, let alone my lady! Now the house ain't that bad, and it won't take a mite to get a room warmed up for you and some hot food in your stomach. Now don't you talk like that ever, Honor Dillard!"

I couldn't keep from smiling; Grace was her old self, bossing me around to make me see her common sense. She was short of stature and very matronly looking since her marriage, but it suited her. Jason, too, had a content look about him, and I guessed they were happy.

"All right," I said, knowing the joy of being home

with Grace again. "Have your own way. But I don't want to insist—"

"Now hush, dearie. Let me hear no more of that! I'll warrant you that Dust and Mrs. Barrows already have a warm fire in your room and food is already being prepared in the kitchen. Jason and I will stay in our own place tonight and move to the house in the morning. But you won't be alone. Mrs. Barrows and Dust will be there. She was just telling me this morning she wished you'd come home so she could be back up in the house again. That cottage is mighty small." She chuckled gently and helped me into my pelisse; I tied on my bonnet.

In a short time we were in the kitchen with Mrs. Barrows and Dust, the housekeeper and Grandfather's "man," who had been his personal valet and butler for as long as I could remember. They had come with my grandfather when he had inherited Friary's Dor from his oldest brother, who had purchased the place from the Quillers. Grandfather Lawrence, my mother's father, had loved the house and grounds because of its antiquity, and he had taught me this love for it, too, while teaching me the arts of healing and caring for the sick.

"Why miss," Mrs. Barrows said, beaming. "You've become a lady now, all grown-up, and a pretty one, too!" She embraced me tightly. A little tub of a Kentish woman, she had brown eyes and wispy dark hair, graying some beneath the white mobcap she wore. "Welcome home, dearie."

"Thank you, Mrs. Barrows," I said. "It's good to be home again."

Dust looked on with a warmth that said he was glad

I was home. His white hair was tied back with a black ribbon, and the pale-blue eyes seemed as bleary looking as they always had. Grandfather had told me he was called Dust because he had always looked dusty.

"It's good to see 'ee, my lady," he said. "Yer rooms'll be warm now as I saw to it myself. It takes a bit to warm up, though, a big house like this'un. But my missus can fix 'ee up a mug o' hot cider."

I smiled at him, knowing again what home-loving people these were and how glad I was to be here among them.

"That sounds like what I've been waiting for, Dust," I laughed lightly. "I've missed our good cider. Nowhere in London do they serve cider like it." This pleased them both, and I continued: "By the way. How are the Pegnallys these days? The cove seemed so isolated, I thought no one was about."

I sensed a hesitation and saw the look of caution pass between husband and wife and Grace, who had been busy taking my pelisse and then setting my place at the big table near the fire.

"Oh, them be well enough, miss," Mrs. Barrows said with hesitation. "T'was most likely you were used to Londontown and the countryside here is quieter."

I laughed again. "That sounds logical, and I'm sure it's the answer. It's just that—well. I remember there seemed to be so much going on down at the winery that even the echo was heard in the cove. I didn't hear that today. But no matter. I'm home now. Where's that hot cider, Mrs. Barrows?"

They seemed relieved, and Mrs. Barrows turned to a pot on the tile stove. "It's simmering, dearie, and I'll just get a mug down now. I've fixed up a batch of hot buttered crumpets, like you always liked, miss. Them'll be ready in no time.

A little later I was eating the light-as-air crumpets and sipping the hot sweet cider. The fire was warm, and I felt safe and secure with these loyal servants who had been a part of my life in the past. Grace sat with me part of the time, talking of the life she and Jason shared; Mrs. Barrows chattered on about the evils of living in a tiny cottage, and between them both I was given quite a picture of how things had been going on here during the past three years.

Friary's Dor had once been a religious establishment of Franciscan Gray Friars, built in the middle fourteenth century and dissolved near the end of the fifteenth when the owners of Quiller Castle bought it. It had then been renovated into a private house, though on a small scale, while the great nave had been left to fall in ruin, as were several other buildings. The chapter house and the monks' dorms and parlor, the infirmary and kitchen, bake house and scullery all around the small enclosed courtyard, and the cloisters in front had been made into a fairly habitable house, a wing added for bedrooms.

Sixty years ago the Quiller family from the castle had sold this portion of land to the Lawrences. My grandfather had told me it was because the former Lord Quiller, Sir Howard, had large gambling debts and needed the money badly. When Grandfather inherited Friary's Dor, he had a small charity hospital going by the time I had come to live here.

The Gray Friars of the fourteenth and fifteenth centuries had cultivated an excellent apple orchard in the dip between the cliffs, and there they had success with

making cider and apple wine in the winery they built
with brick among the orchards. Because they had built
the friary with the winery in mind, the secret caves
were excellent for their own shipping. The cove was so
hidden that the tuns could be stored in the caves for
illicit smuggling to the French coast. Those friars had
no qualms about this form of trade, but then, so said
Grandfather, neither had the Quillers while they had
owned the Dor.

There was a legend about Friary's Dor, and the
name itself suggested the legend was true. *Dor* meant
trick, a Cornish word, and it came about after the friary had been abandoned and sold.

The legend states that one of the friars in the fifteenth century went mad after he sold his soul to the
Devil, who then was living at the castle just newly
built. The Devil had wanted to own the friary, but the
friars refused to sell it on any condition. Knowing that
the dissolution was headed their way, that one greedy
friary bargained with the Devil at the castle and sold
the friary to Him.

The brothers learned of this betrayal and locked him
in the tower that overlooked the Channel. Then they
fled, and the friary was abandoned. Several years afterward the Quiller family bought the religious establishment from the Crown. When the tower was opened,
there were no remains of a body except the cowled
robe lying there. It was said the ghost of that friar
haunted the Quiller family; unexplained tragedies occurred every year; misfortunes struck, and the great
Quiller estate dwindled.

Witnesses verified they saw a Gray Friar walk
through the mists along the chalk cliffs and around the
old tower every December when those tragedies hap-

pened at the castle less than two miles away. However, when the friary was sold to the Lawrences, these misfortunes ceased, and it was said the mad friar had not been seen since that time.

I never believed the legend when I was a child. But according to the servants and the villagers, servants had been hard to keep at the Dor and at the castle.

It was late when I stirred from that warm kitchen, warmed by the comfort of Grace and Mrs. Barrows. I had always been treated as one of them, and not as a mistress they would have to answer to some day. This night, I knew as they did that this situation would soon be altered with the arrival of my father.

When I awakened the following morning, a red sun was veiled by the mists that always came in late November. I had always loved the autumns here on the Kentish coast, and I slipped out of bed and hurried to the windows. The diamond panes were heavily leaded, narrow and long, and I flung them wide open and looked out. The smell of burning leaves from the orchards was in the air, along with the nip that made my skin tingle.

I breathed in the delicious air and heard the sounds coming from other parts of the house. The servants were already busy, I thought, gazing out across the turf toward the old friars' tower I had passed the night before.

The cove was hidden from the house; in fact, it was so hidden that no one knew of its existence unless he were familiar with the grounds.

My thoughts were on the ship I'd seen in the cove last night, *The Dark Lady.* Were the servants aware of its existence? Had that look I'd seen pass between

Dust and his wife been significant?

Most assuredly, I knew the man I'd encountered had been connected with *The Dark Lady,* and I wondered if I'd ever see him again. I turned back to my room, hugging that thought to me guiltily.

I washed in the bowl with the daisy garlands on it and dressed in one of my oldest gowns, a dark blue sarcenet with long sleeves. I wondered if Grace had seen the threadbare condition of my clothes; all those lovely gowns that had been made for me at Madam Claude's three years ago were now worn and patched and thin. I leaned forward to look at myself in the mirror as I finished brushing and braiding my hair.

It was nearly black, with just a tinge of red and much too long to wear in a topknot of curls, so fashionable these days. I was not delicately boned, either; my face had a strong look about it, with dark eyebrows over slightly tilted gray eyes, and my complexion was much too healthy looking to be in the height of fashion.

I was not short, but not tall, either, rather slenderly built, and I could wear the flowing tunic gowns very well without having to look plump, as so many of the ladies did in them. Madam Claude had assured me of this. With that in mind, I left the room.

Mrs. Barrows placed a plate of eggs and bacon in front of me along with a steaming cup of coffee. I told her of Father's intentions to come to Friary's Dor, but I didn't know when. "I know it will take some doing to get the house in order, but you can get help from the village if you like," I said. "The house must be cleaned. I'm sure you must recall how my father is!" I laughed, swallowing some coffee.

"And that I do, miss," she said. "He were quite set

on things being orderly and all, if I remember correctly. But then that were because of his life with the army, were it not? I remember Lady Cathy—Miss Cathy to us, your dear mother, miss. She always smiled and said Sir Reginald was too orderly to have a wife properly, but I knew that she were excusing him because she loved him. Not that Miss Cathy weren't orderly herself. She did have neat ways, if I do recall." She sighed.

She placed a plate of hot cross buns in front of me. "You do favor her, miss. I told Dust last night that you look just like our Miss Cathy, now that you're grown up and come back. Grace tells us that you're here to stay. May I say that pleases both Dust and myself?"

I glanced up at her over the brim of my coffee cup. "Why Mrs. Barrows! That is the nicest compliment I know of. You must believe me. I, too, am glad to be home. I should never have gone away."

Just at that moment the door opened, and Grace came in with two young maids behind her. "Good morning, Honor," Grace breezed in. "I came by the winery and brought up the twins to help out with the cleaning. You remember the Pegnally girls." She took off her gray cloak and bonnet and hung them behind the door.

Of course I recognized them; Meg and Peg—they would be fifteen now, I thought, as my glance went over their overripe bodies, which suggested they were older. They were look-alikes, but I knew Meg had darker hair than Peg, and Peg had freckles sprinkled lightly across her nose, which gave her that pert look her father, Tom Pegnally, had.

"Girls, this is Miss Honor." Grace said.

"How you've both grown!" I said, smiling at them, remembering the days when I had played with them down at the winery. "I suspect your brother Tommy is a man now if this is how you both have shot up." We laughed easily together. Tommy was one year younger than myself, and I had just turned twenty in October.

"Oh yes, miss," Peg cried, bobbing a half-curtsy, holding out the full blue wool skirt with one hand. "He's a right big man now, but we ain't seen him for several months. He went to Londontown."

"Oh. I didn't know that, Peg. I suppose your parents are missing him dreadfully down at the winery." I recalled how Tom had wanted his son to take over the wine- and cider-making as he himself had done.

"Tommy! That one!" exclaimed Meg, wrinkling her nose. "He would have none of it, so he went to London. Father says to let him go now and sow his wild oats, and then he be settled later in life." This bit of wisdom would have struck me as comical had it not been so seriously said, and Grace hushed her with: "Well, we'd better get started with this cleaning. Oh, Honor," she said, hurrying to her cloak, "a letter just came for you by post. Jason brought it up from Peacock's cot where the mail coach stopped earlier. It's from Sir Reginald."

She handed me the letter, and I heard her talking to the girls as they left the room. Surprised, I sat at the table for a moment before opening it. How on earth did Father know I was here? How could he possibly know so soon? I stared down at the envelope addressed: Honor Dillard. Friary's Dor, Friarsgate Village, Kent.

CHAPTER THREE

THE letter was brusque and to the point. "I'm return-
ing at once to England via Dover. Please have the
house presentable as I am bringing a guest. I suggest
you remain there at Friary's Dor. I will arrive sometime during first week in December to settle your future." It was signed, "Sir Reginald, Colonel Dillard,
52nd Regiment."

I placed the letter in the pocket of my gown and
grabbed a dark woolen cloak from the back hall parlor and went out of the house. There was hardly more
than a fortnight before he was to arrive, I thought,
counting the days in my mind. I would have to sort out
my thoughts, make plans and somehow gain the courage I needed to face Father and say "No" to any of his
"arrangements."

Father knew Friary's Dor was mine; it had been
willed to me by Grandfather. Father had his own
manor, Gardencroft House in Sussex, and in this I
would give him no anxiety. All I wanted was to live
here in my own house, open the hospital again, and
care for the sick as Grandfather had done.

As I left the cloisters, I enjoyed the way the trees of
the orchards formed a lacy pattern against the blue
sky, and the mellow scent of apples from the winery

was like the wine itself made by Tom and Moll Pegnally.

The sea was pellucid green; the sunlight muted on everything a tinge of gold. I walked down to the cove, but there was no trace of the ship, *The Dark Lady*. I hadn't expected to see it, but nevertheless I was curious. It all might have been a dream, I thought, as I stared at that sparkling water had I not kept the musket ball I had dug from the man's flesh. It was hidden among my personal things.

I strolled down to the quay, then turned and went up the brick path that led to the winery itself. I had always loved coming here; the old building was partially covered with ivy creeper now scarlet, the vines virtually hiding the dark red brick.

The wing in which the Pegnallys lived was more like a large farmhouse, the main building rising behind it, housing the offices and the giant wooden casks with ladders leading to catwalks overhead. Beyond this was the vast wine-press building; I knew, for I had been here often when the wine was being made.

I went through a stone-floored wash house into a flagstone passage and knocked on a heavy oak door. It was flung open by little Robbie, the ten-year-old son, who stood staring at me shyly. Moll Pegnally, who was scrubbing potatoes in a large copper basin, turned.

"Well," she said, wiping her hands on the apron over her rust-colored woolen gown, "bless me if it ain't Miss Honor come back! My dear life, we do be honored, miss. Come in. There, Robbie, bring up a chair like a good boy that you are—the good one if you please, so our miss can be comfortable-like."

Moll Pegnally was a gypsy woman who married Tom in spite of all the oppositions. She was still a good-looking raven-haired woman whose dark eyes matched those of her daughters, Meg and Peg. Her tanned skin was still firm, and her teeth were good and strong, which made her smile easy and infectious.

"You haven't change a bit, Mrs. Pegnally," I said, accepting the chair Robbie brought and thanking him. "But I hardly recognized the twins; they've grown up, and so has Robbie!" I smiled at the little ruddy-cheeked boy, noticing his fine but shy dark eyes. "And the twins tell me Tommy has left."

She laughed. "Oh, he has at that, miss, but it won't be for long. I know my son, and he won't put up with what Londontown will do to him." She chuckled in a low husky voice. "He'll be back before Christmas, I tell my family. My, but you could've knocked me over with a feather when Mrs. Dare came down this morning to fetch the twins to the house and told me you was home! And no word that you was coming!"

"Yes, it was rather sudden. My coming home, I mean." I waited a moment. "How's Tom doing? One of the things I missed was the fresh sweet smells of his cider-making, not to mention it's taste. I'm glad to be home."

"Aye, and that you would, dearie, you would," she said, sympathetic. "My Tom is in the cider room today, as I know you can smell it miles around. He misses Tommy, though. You can tell that. He seems sort of anxious-like, but he'll snap out of it in time."

I gazed around the room, familiar even now. It had two large windows, rather narrow and latticed, an open fireplace as well as the large oven, red tiles, and the huge trestle table in the center where we sat at one end. On the oak beams hung a ham, sides of bacon, and bundles of herbs. Near the window was a large oak cask, iron-bound, and it had always been full of good sweet cider for the family. The room and its scents were a part of my life, just as the sea and chalk cliffs were. I felt at home here.

Moll had been kind to me when I was a girl. Grandfather had told me she was a good wife to Tom and that in spite of her being a gypsy who once had worked in the hop fields of Kent, she had settled with Tom as a right kind of wife for him. He didn't explain that, but I knew what he'd meant.

She had told my fortune once—only once—and I recalled I thought it had been done in fun at the time because she had vowed she would never practice her gypsy way of life and its spells when she married.

That day long ago, when I was sixteen, she had grabbed my hand and looked at my palm. She had said: "You're going to marry for love, miss, but you are a very stubborn young girl, and it won't be easy. There is a long voyage, dark and dangerous. Don't be fooled by the wrong man in your life." She had dropped my hand, then had laughed her unrestrained gypsy laugh, and soon it was forgotten.

Now I said: "So Tom is busy today?" She placed two tankards of cider on the table and sat down across from me. "I suppose he's getting a fair local price for it still? What with the export tax it must be difficult to get it abroad to the Continent. Tom wouldn't think of smuggling, would he, Mrs. Pegnally?"

She stared at me, her dark eyes unreadable. "Smuggling, miss? Why I never heard of such a thing that my Tom would do like that, it being against the law and all, miss. How come you ask such a thing?"

"Smuggling is not new, not here at Friary's Dor, by any means, Mrs. Pegnally," I said softly. "Those old

Gray Friars did illicit trade from the first, and their consciences never hurt. I'm told the Quiller family, when they owned the Dor, had no qualms about it. It is being done all along the coast, you see." I gazed at her over the brim of my mug while I tasted the cider.

She was silent a moment, then replied, "Why, miss, times do be hard, t'is true, and like as not t'will be so for some time to come, what with that French war going on like it is. But we've enough problems here with the local tax to be counted by them revenuers. That's why my Tommy left here. He was tired of having to say 'yes, sir' and 'no, sir' to them ever' time he went in with the casks. My Tom keeps the law, miss, he does." She was defiant, as I knew she would be.

It was no coincidence that I'd seen that ship in the cove and had the encounter with that man. Tom Pegnally had to know it had been anchored there, for the cove could be seen clearly and close from the winery even in a heavy mist. Naturally, Moll would defend him, and I knew I would, too. Well, so be it, I thought, licking my lips with my tongue. I was not going to tell anyone—not even my father when he arrived. I would simply keep my eyes open.

I said: "I'm sure Tom does all right, Mrs. Pegnally. He's a good man. My grandfather had a lot of trust in him, and I do, too." My voice was low. I wanted her to know I understood. "By the way. My father is coming to Friary's Dor sometime in December."

I watched the effect this news had on her. "Sir Reginald coming here, miss? But I thought—we all thought he was in that country fighting the French general, Bonaparte!"

"Oh yes. He's doing his part in Portugal, but he will come home for a few weeks. I believe he feels he has

some business to look after. I received a letter from
him this morning confirming the first week in December. I'm glad Grace thought to get your girls to help
out at the house. My father is a fanatic on order and
cleanliness." I laughed lightly.

She seemed to laugh from within. "Lordy, that he
would come here at this time," she said, almost as if to
herself. "Well I'll get my Tom to give the old place a
scrubbing down. It needs it, too, now that the season is over." We heard a dull thumping sound.

She stood up and looked out the window. "I reckon
that'll be Peacock coming down for some more peat
for his greenhouse. You know his daughter and her husband left and went to Londontown, too, oh some time
last spring. Peacock is worried silly about them, for not
long ago a wandering gypsy man came through here
and left a message from her. He said them are dying
like flies on the streets o' London for want of food and
such. It do sound bad, now, don't it?" I guessed she
was thinking of Tommy.

"Did the message give Peacock any news of Letty?"

"Oh, it said she weren't feeling too good but for
them not to worry none." We were silent for a while,
and then I stood up to take my leave. I would have to
go down to Peacock's cottage and pay a visit to him
and his wife. I remembered how much the old man
doted on his only daughter; the man she had married
was worthless, so everyone said, and now it seemed as
if it might have been true.

Moll, standing with her shapely body outlined in the
rust-colored woolen gown and white apron, watched
me go from the door.

The housecleaning was thorough; I helped by dusting the heavy books in the library; that room had been the old chapter house originally, an irregularly shaped room with a wide stone fireplace at one end and two walls covered with leather-bound books on its shelves.

The carpets were frayed and quite faded, but once they were dusted and the floors polished, as well as the furniture and ceiling beams, it was presentable. Between the library and the great hall was the large stone parlor the friars once used for seeing their visitors. Now it was simply used as the entry hall; in here, too, was a wide stone fireplace in which Dust kept a fire going most of the time, for the house was otherwise damp and cold. The great hall was not used except when company came and on Christmas, but it, too, had been cleaned beyond recognition when we finished three days later.

When I took the final tour through the house, I was indeed surprised, as well as pleased, with the accomplishments. I overlooked the threadbare, but still beautiful, gold velvet curtains in the library. To me Friary's Dor had more than beauty; it was a home I cherished, and I didn't want to change even the frayed part.

To my father Friary's Dor had been nothing but a pile of old stones, crumbling to ruin. He had never been able to stay for long periods. "I can't abide this isolation, nor the ruinious state it's in," I used to hear him say, and he always had an excuse to leave before his appointed time.

Father was a stern man; I had never been able to call him the genteel title of "Papa" even when I was a child and living with him and my mother in Calcutta, India. His own father, an illustrious man of naval background, had seen to it my father was brought up with strict military form. It suited him, I thought, and he

was as illustrious as Grandfather Dillard had been.
With four years behind him on the battlefield against
Napoleon Bonaparte in Spain, Father had made a
name for himself.

Certainly the servants here at Friary's Dor stood in
awe of him, though they didn't particularly like him.
They had felt a keen sense of loyalty to Grandfather
Lawrence, and when I had come here to live, they had
accepted me as a Lawrence rather than a Dillard. But
everyone had to admire Father. He was stern but just,
and I knew it. The servants feared him, too, after a
fashion, knowing he demanded obedience to the
law, and when a job was ordered to be done, they
knew just how well done he wanted it.

When the servants learned Father was coming to
Friary's Dor, even down to the small tenant farms,
they speeded up lagging chores, and I suspected they
recalled all too clearly the last visit Father had made
here three years ago.

The days sped by quickly; they were pleasant, and
I found myself, more often than not, walking down on
the chalk cliffs in the lingering late November days.
Some days the French coast was visible, but on others
the mists hid that coastline in a fine blue haze.

My thoughts were constantly on the man I had met
that first night. I tried hard to put him from my mind;
I believed he had to be acquainted with this coast to
know of Friars Cove, not to mention that he was known
by the Pegnallys as well.

I felt uneasy one evening when I returned to the
house and saw Moll had been watching me in a secre-
tive manner. Perhaps I was too sensitive, knowing the
danger I had been in a few weeks ago. A spy; was that
not in character, spying and being spied on?

The day my father arrived, it was shortly after noon, and when the landau pulled up into the courtyard, two alert grooms jumped down and opened the door. I watched from above, as I was in my grandfather's bed-room, sorting out some old medical books.

I was astonished to see that his guest was a lady, bringing with her a foreign-looking abigail. The lady was dressed in a soft blue velvet pelisse and bonnet, which hid her face momentarily from me, as she was directly below. Father handled her as if she were the most precious possession on earth.

I simply stared until they disappeared inside the doorway beneath me, and only then did I leave the room, slowly making my way down the stairs. I took care to glance at myself in a mirror to see if my hair was in place and that there were no dust smudges on my face or gown. I had thought to wear my second-best gown—the gray muslin Madam Claude had called *London fog*—embroidered with pale pink roses on the hem and around the neckline. It was tied with a pink satin ribbon; still, it was threadbare and thin, but it would serve its purpose for this meeting with my father and his guest.

When I descended to the parlor, Dust had already shown Father and the lady into the library, the abigail waiting down the hall. Dust was in his best livery, a faded and somewhat out-of-date affair of pale blue, his buckled shoes polished and his white hair tied back with ribbon.

"He be asking fer 'ee, my lady," he whispered, his lower lip protruding as it always did whenever he was perplexed. "Better 'ee go in," and he opened the door for me.

Father, still in his colorful cape, which covered the

uniform of buff facing and silver lace of the 52nd Regiment, was standing near the lady who had accompanied him, and they both turned as I entered.

He was a good-looking man in his early forties; ramrod straight, his dark brown hair, without a trace of gray, was still thick above his lean tanned face; his gray-blue eyes were bluer now than I remembered them and brilliant in the afternoon sunlight that fell through the windows in golden shafts. There was a pleased expression on his face, and an odd amusement played around his mouth.

"Honor, my dear," he said, not moving toward me, "I want you to meet Cecily—my wife."

Sheer surprise left me speechless. I couldn't imagine Father being married to anyone, so I simply stared. It was an awkward moment.

Finally I managed: "Your wife, Father?" My voice was barely audible, hesitant.

"Yes. My wife." His voice was full of tenderness as he glanced down at her. He didn't seem to mind the awkward moment; if he felt it, he gave no indication. She had taken off her bonnet and pelisse, and was looking at me through the bluest of eyes; they were long-lashed and wide-set in a face that was oval-shaped and fair. Her dark blonde hair shone like strained honey above the blue of her gown. She resembled a Dresden china doll, a fragile and delicate beauty.

Father said: "Cecily, I know you and Honor will be friends. This is my daughter."

She reached out and took my hand in hers. "I do hope we'll be very close friends, Honor," she said in a voice that was as sweet as she looked. Her face was slightly flushed, and the warmth of her color was heightened from the pink lips to the dark-lashed blue eyes.

"I'm sure we can," I stammered. "I had no idea—It was a surprise," I finished lamely, completely at a loss for words.

"I can see that it is a surprise—a shocking surprise," she agreed. "We should have told her, Reggie darling," she said, looking up at Father, her voice gentle.

"There wasn't time, and besides, my daughter was not available if I recall correctly. But no matter now. I know you'll want to go to our rooms to rest some, and Dust will show you there. I must discuss a matter of importance with Honor. I'll be up later, my darling."

I simply couldn't believe this was my father talking. Dust, too, was still standing directly behind me, and he found it hard to accept. But he moved forward and said: "This way, my lady."

Cecily put a soft delicate hand to Father's cheek. "Don't be too hard on her, Reggie. She seems so young. Youth is always so impetuous. Remember that."

"I shall, Cecily," Father said, relinquishing her to Dust, admonishing him with: "See to it my lady has all her needs, Dust. Perhaps some light refreshment—"

"Now darling, don't spoil me so," she said, laughing. "I shall be quite all right. Dust will show me the way, and I shall endeavor to make myself pleasant while you two are discussing . . . family business." She smiled at him—for him, I should say, then turned and left the room with Dust who closed the door behind them.

CHAPTER FOUR

FATHER gestured to me to be seated on the rose brocade sofa facing the fireside and stood as if he were waiting. I wondered suddenly if he had found out about my part of being a spy. Surely he could not have done so?

"I'm sorry I had to spring this surprise on you in this manner, Honor. To tell the truth, there wasn't much time, and it is still a wonder—a most fantastic wonder —to find myself married, and to Cecily. She is everything to me, all I could desire, and that she chose me—" He stopped abruptly, looked abashed for a moment that he should have disclosed his thoughts to me. But I could not have been so astonished myself, hearing it.

"Isn't she lovely? Do you think so, Honor?" His voice was tender but anxious, his eyes full and vivid upon my face.

Stunned that he should even consider my opinion, I hastily said: "By all means, she is very beautiful, Father. When did you get married?"

"In Portugal, where she was staying with friends and some relatives who had followed the regiment to Lisbon. We met three months ago, but she consented to be my wife just two weeks ago, and that is why I

had no time to let anyone know, you see. She is part French," he said anxiously. "We shall be living in Dover now; as soon as my assignment comes through, that is. Well. Enough of that. How have you been, Honor?" He lifted his eyebrows inquiringly.

I averted his gaze for a moment. "Fairly well, Father, thank you."

"Hm-mn, I see. Well. I came down here for the sole purpose of seeing to your future. Lady Deveril was very exasperated with you. She hinted that there was very little else she could do for you, and she felt you would be leaving her soon. Do you care to tell me about it?"

I raised my eyes to his. "I left London because I tired of that useless way of living, Father. I came home, and I'm staying here for good."

"Hm-mn, and Cecily would have loved that London society you so spurn. What do you see in this heap of ruins?" He glanced around the room and then back at me, his hands behind his back, his shoulders straight.

I opened my mouth to speak, but he cut in: "Well, it's your liking, though I don't understand it. I've given you the opportunity most young ladies would love to have."

"I'm grateful, too, Father," I murmured.

"Are you, my dear girl? You didn't take the advantage to use for choosing a suitable husband, and so I've made the arrangements for you. I'm certain you will agree with them in the end. You have behaved very unseemly, running off the way you did from Lady Deveril's generous care. I sometimes wonder if she hadn't been your mother's best friend . . . Well. There's no need to tell you it was all uncalled for."

"I won't have my life arranged for me, Father," I said heatedly.

He stared at me for one long moment. "Now I tell you this. I know how you feel toward this decayed ruins, that you call home. To my way of thinking, it should have been sold long ago, but of course I made a promise to your Grandfather Lawrence that it should be yours." He seemed to have ignored my outburst of defiance and went on.

"Here are the way things stand. Because this land once belonged to the castle, it is quite natural that Lord Quiller wishes to see it regained into their family. Lord Quiller has no immediate heirs, that is to say, sons, but he has a nephew, and this nephew has consented to an arrangement; he will marry you. I want to see you married. Lord Quiller has promised his nephew the Quiller estate upon his death if he marries now. The stipulations are that if you consent to marry the nephew, Friary's Dor will remain yours, to be given to your heirs. At the same time, you will be secure in a good family with a husband, while the land goes back into the Quiller estate."

I stared at him, almost unable to believe what he was saying. I found my voice: "You—"

Seeing my expression, he held up a hand, and I was sure he knew what was passing through my mind. "The nephew, Heath Quiller, will inherit the title when he marries but not the castle until his uncle's death. I believe he is a young man in his late twenties. I haven't met him, but that is being arranged."

Heath Quiller! I thought incredulously. Who hadn't heard of him? His name was linked with the French, and he was once a friend of Napoleon Bonaparte! His own family had disowned him because of his open re-

bellion and reportedly scandalous affairs with some
French woman.

I glared at my father. "How could you make a bargain when you had nothing to bargain with?" I asked,
despising him at that moment. "You had no right to
barter my life, to do this contemptible thing without
my consent! Friary's Dor isn't yours—it's mine, and
you are aware of this!" I didn't recognize my voice.

"Honor, you are overdramatic. Surely you knew I
was the sole holder for the estate of your grandfather?
He would have lost it long ago to his creditors had I
not bought it outright for him and saved it for you. I
might remind you of that. And that proves my point
right there, young lady. Had you been a shrewd busi-
nesswoman, you would have found out about it. You
need someone to look after you and this place. The up-
keep is tremendous, and in spite of the fact that I kept
my solemn promise to your grandfather, there is no
way you can cope with it outside of marriage. As I
see it, Honor, you have nothing to lose if you consent
to this marriage. This place will be yours entirely, to
do as you will when you are married. Those are the
terms."

"And the nephew? After the marriage what's to
prevent him from taking it from me at his will, as you
have seen fit to do? Won't I be considered his *chattel*?"
I was bitter. "He seems so willing to marry me, to gain
possession of my property. Where, then, will be my
rights?" I stood up, defiant, blind with tears of anger
and hate.

"You are far too emotional to see this rationally. You
won't be his . . . *chattel*, as you call it. I told you, the
stipulations are that you will be the owner of Friary's
Dor. It's in your name, and I might add, there is no

way that it can be taken from you or your heirs if you marry Heath Quiller."

"How could you do this, knowing—" I turned, my eyes blazing at him, my fists clenched.

He came and faced me, placing his hands on my shoulders. I shrank from his touch, but he did not seem to notice. "You mustn't think of it like that, Honor. I have your best interest at heart, and believe me, you will benefit from this marriage."

"And if I refuse?" I was defiant.

He dropped his hands. "Then, my dear, you will lose Friary's Dor. I will sell it right out from under you. I might warn you now—" There was a hint of steel in his voice that chilled my heart. "There will be no carrying on as if I've deprived you of something. You're considered grown-up now, and I expect you to conduct yourself in that manner. The arrangements have been prepared, and the papers are all in order. The young man has been out of the country and is due back sometime this week. I shall be notified of the matter, and then we shall proceed at once. I believe a New Year's wedding is what we have in mind."

I could hardly breathe, so great was the shock.

Father must have sensed this, for he said in a more congenial tone: "I took the liberty while I was in London last week to have your wedding clothes ordered. Madam Claude gladly took the order, as she has your correct fittings. Your trousseau, with the gracious help of Lady Deveril has also been ordered. I trust they will be suitable. The gown will be sent directly to my quarters, of course, for you will be joining me there. But your new trousseau will arrive here in a day or two."

I couldn't think of anything suitable to say except, "Thank you, Father."

"That's my duty as well as a father's pleasure, Honor. I take it, then, that you consent to the arrangements?"

I glanced up at him, knowing my eyes mirrored my feelings, and then lowered them to my hands clasped tightly in front of me as I sat down again. "I have no choice, have I? I must consent, or . . ." My voice was barely audible.

"You are wise to consent. With the money Heath Quiller will bring here you may be able to salvage this relic of the past, preserve all these stones that should have been torn down long ago," he chuckled. "I understand from Lord Quiller that the nephew is anxious —almost as anxious as you are, my girl, to preserve this old religious haunt. I had no idea that he knew it so well, but then, it's not unusual; the castle is close enough."

I felt a repulsion for the man in question. "What does he do for a living, Father?"

"I understand he works for the Home Office, an agent in the Diplomatic Corps. He has a ship called *The Blue Star*, and at one time it was a merchant ship, I believe. I'm surprised you didn't meet him in London at some of those fancy affairs. His parents have a town house there. Have you met him?"

"No. But I have heard certain rumors about him—" I stopped, seeing the expression on his face.

He chuckled low, almost as if he thought it a jest. He clasped his hands behind his back again and smiled amicably. "You must not believe every rumor you hear of gentlemen, Honor. I'll warrant you, he may have been around, but I would put it from my mind in the future, if I were in your place, to be wise. Let me give you a piece of advice, for what it's worth, Honor. Don't begrudge Heath Quiller his past. He is entitled to it as much as you are to yours."

It was a clear evening, and the full moon was just tipping the horizon over the Channel when I left the house and strolled along the chalk cliffs. Father and Cecily had gone to their rooms; earlier, I had seen the servants gathered in the library and guessed that Father was instructing them, giving them the news of the pending marriage.

Now the moon was rising like a luminous silk ball, making a golden pathway on the sea. Down below me the crystal ocean met the shore and splashed lacy foam on the glistening white chalk.

A cold, gentle breeze was blowing. I could not see the lights on the distant French coast because I knew the inevitable mists would hide them; almost too soon, as if by cue, wisps of silvery vapor began to trail across the ultramarine sky, and it was then I saw the shape and form of a ship on that sea, gliding into the path the moon made. For a while it was silhouetted between sky and sea, its sails billowed out in perfect form.

Then she did a strange turn and silently, stealthily stole in toward the cliffs. To my astonishment it slipped lithely between the cliffs into the cove beyond me to the right. A strange elation possessed me suddenly. Could it be *The Dark Lady*?

It was important to me to find out, and I hurried back along the path until I could glimpse the cove easily without being seen. Experience cautioned me to be careful, and it was then I saw someone on the quayside with a lantern directing the ship into the cove. There were no lights aboard the dark ship, and I heard no sounds.

The breeze had begun to stir up at this height, and I couldn't see the name of the ship from here, nor did I wish to take a chance on being seen. So I retraced my steps and went back to the house, knowing that I truly should report this to my father.

He had given me permission to stay on at Friary's Dor without his presence for the next week or two, and I wished it to remain like that; if I told him, he would not let me stay, no matter what happened. So I went to my room and stood at the casement, staring out at the old tower. If the ship was *The Dark Lady,* I was certain that *he* would be aboard her. Would he come up to the infirmary this time?

Suddenly I heard a low whistle almost directly under my window. I leaned over to see a figure stealing out from the shadows of the house and hurrying across the turf to the tower where another dark figure stood waiting. The one crossing the turf raised his hand as if in a warning.

I stepped back into the folds of the curtain, my long hair falling over my body, and my breath quickened. The two men stood together for some time, and I guessed a person from that ship had been warned by someone from the house.

Who could it be? A curious excitement mingled with a sense of danger filled me. It was like old times when Anthony used to call me out from Lady Deveril's house at midnight for the information I had to give him.

Now I was curious to know more. It was most likely to be Tom Pegnally, for Jason was not that tall, nor could Dust run like that. I had overheard Father talking to Tom about the smuggling, and I guessed Tom had to warn the ship's crew of Father's presence.

I wanted more than anything to see that man again; yet what could I say to him? Wouldn't it prove embarrassing now?

The two shadows disappeared down the path to the cove. The mists had already begun to steal in, and there was no sound anywhere. I went to bed then, but it was some time before I finally fell asleep.

Early the next morning I went down to breakfast and was told that my father had already eaten and was now in the library with a visitor. Lady Dillard was still in her rooms. The door between the dining room and library was open, and I heard a man with a querulous voice say:

"Confound it, Reginald. This scoundrel, a notorious one at that, a Captain Dark, he's called, is getting away with murder along this coast, and no one has been able to catch him! Every conceivable crime in the book could be thrown at him if he were captured, I dare say!"

Father laughed dryly, and I thought they would be entering the room, so I prepared myself for it. But they did not.

"A sly fox, eh, Mark? Well, he'll be caught in due time. There's no evidence that he's been seen around here, but then I don't intend to believe all the denials the servants give." He laughed again, and a short silence followed.

The other man went on to say: "The way that Captain Dark eludes the revenue agents is a complete mystery, Reginald. He's swift and sly, does it under cover. They're saying he's a slaver, too, making his runs to Spanish America with them. This I don't know, it's only hearsay. But I'm anxious to have him caught. Percival is, too. Hang it all, I've word that Captain Dark has been hired by the merchants in every southern town along this coast to make those illegal runs for them, and of course that's his secret of success. And how he does it, or when he does it, no one knows! He's like a dark ghost, and he'll go down as a legend!"

Father laughed. "There are plenty of inlets and estuaries he could use, Mark. But he'll be caught one of these days. That kind always outsmart themselves."

"I hope you're right," the man said. Then after a hesitation:

"How is that pretty bride of yours, Reginald?"

"She's weary of this isolated ruin I've brought her to, Mark. And I can't really blame her. I'm glad we're going into Margate today. Thank God my orders came early this morning. I'm pleased with my assignment—couldn't have asked for a better one right now than at the Margate Garrison. I'll be able to conduct that marriage of my daughter to your nephew without danger of her running away or backing out at the last moment. But she did consent, and I don't think she will change her mind."

I nearly choked on my coffee.

"Good, good. I'm relieved that Heath came home yesterday at last. I came over here as soon as I could to let you know. So you'll be going into Margate today?"

"Just as soon as the grooms have the landau ready and the ensign who brought my orders has had his breakfast, Mark. And of course my wife is now in preparation to leave. She perked up when I told her the good news. I think she is frightened of this place.

It has something to do with her tragic childhood, I believe, when the terrorists took her father and mother
to the guillotine." He sighed heavily.

"Ah yes. That was a tragic time for the innocent." I
heard them move away from the door, and their voices
faded.

CHAPTER FIVE

I SUSPECTED the servants were relieved when Father took his new wife to Margate, and after they'd gone, I fancied their attitudes were different toward me.

Father had mentioned I was to plan on a visit to Margate in two or three days time, with Grace and Jason accompanying me, and I guessed it was to meet Heath Quiller and to sign the final papers.

That same afternoon I walked down into the village. I had gone down to the cove earlier, to see if that ship were still there, but it was gone, and it might have been a dream had I not seen it with my own eyes. I was aware of keen disappointment, and I think it was that which confirmed my decision to go into Friarsgate.

The air had a nip in it, tingling my skin as I walked along the cliff path by the sea. The low hedgerows dipped down beside the path, and I saw the lacy patterns the cobwebs formed over them. Gulls cried and wheeled out over the peacock-blue sea, and the French coast was visible, the faraway white cliffs gleaming in the clear day.

Friarsgate was a tiny fishing village nestled right down on the shale; it was an old village, with an air of a world away, being bypassed by the Dover road. It had a large Norman church and a crooked narrow cobblestone street with tiny Tudor shops and houses right on the waterfront where the ships were tied up.

Today the Dover sole and cat and dogfish scents mingled in the salty sea air with dried kelp. A few fishermen were mending their nets in the sun; others were bringing in lobster pots. This was a familiar scene to me, but always fascinating. I was certain no one would recognize me now from the young girl who used to tag along with Doctor Lawrence.

Little had changed, but I did notice a shop I'd not seen before—a book shop sandwiched in between the jeweler's and the tobacco shop. I decided I would browse around in it, so I opened the door and stepped inside. It was a cheery place, a frayed but bright carpet on the floor and shelves of books, old and new.

There were not many people in the shop, and the proprietor, a wizened little old man who peered out from behind quaint spectacles on his nose, was new to the village, too, or he was new to me.

He was at the counter in the back of the room talking with a customer whose back was to me. I saw only the back of her head, and if I noticed the rich color of her glossy red-gold curls against the vibrant green of her fashionable cloak and bonnet, I'm not sure. It was only when she asked the proprietor if he knew Mister Heath Quiller and where the Quiller Castle was that I turned and stared, and really saw her.

The proprietor shook his head: "I'm new here, my lady, and I don't know many people. The castle, now, is a few miles up the hill on the coast, but t'is Lord Mark Quiller who lives there. Him and his Lady Quiller."

"Where can I hire a gig or carriage to take me there?" Her voice carried an inflection of rudeness, I thought, impatient for having been denied the answers she wished. Her accent was French, which disturbed me somehow.

"Yon's the stable, miss. Old Mister Bell will direct you, I should think." He pointed toward the livery across the street.

Without murmuring even a polite "thank you," she turned and brushed past me angrily. It was then I saw the dark-lashed green eyes flashing in a face so beautiful I knew I would never forget it.

She barely saw me, if at all, but I didn't care. I knew only that she knew Heath Quiller and that she was here to see him! I guessed that she was one of his mistresses, no doubt the latest one! So he was that kind of man, I thought, to have the women running after him!

I was so angry that I turned and stalked out of the shop, a sense of injustice raging within me. I walked briskly toward the waterfront, my mood for shopping wrung from me. How I wished I could somehow escape my fate! What a detestable future I had to face. To marry a man who would no doubt flaunt his mistress in my face from time to time was worse than anything I could have bargained for.

I was almost overcome with my emotion when I glanced up and saw someone directly in front of me blocking my way. Stunned, I realized who it was, and I simply stood there and stared.

"So we meet again, Miss Dillard," he said, laughing, his dark eyes on my face. "But—" He glanced around us, and before I could protest, he took my arm and turned me toward the lane that led out of the village. "I simply don't like to stand on a street and talk," he said, "and I do want to talk with you. Something has upset you. Did I shock you?"

"I—I never expected to—" I stopped.

"You never expected to see me, and so soon. Ah, but I had to come back. But tell me. Has your father come home?"

I stammered: "Ye-ss, he has." How on earth could he know I was upset?

He laughed. "I saw it in your face, Miss Dillard," he said, almost as if he'd read my thoughts. "I thought as much. Would you like to talk about it? Has he presented his arranged plans to you for your future?"

My cheeks burned hotly with embarrassment. "I'm surprised that you would remember."

He cocked an eyebrow at me, and I was aware of his lean tanned face close to mine. "As I recall, you were quite vehement against any arrangement for your future, Miss Dillard. I couldn't forget that. Did you have the courage to stand up to Sir Reginald Dillard, a colonel in the mighty 52nd Regiment?" There was that glimmer of secret laughter in his eyes as they met mine.

I averted his gaze, knowing a sense of ecstasy mingled with loss. "No. Of course I didn't have the courage, if you must know the truth. It's more than I bargained for, you see. I could do nothing about it."

We were silent for a while. "Would you care to tell me about it? I'd like to hear, you see." His voice was gentle. I looked at him for a while, wondering why he chose to be interested. It was enough, however, that he was interested, so I told him.

"It's ironic," I said. "I must marry to keep my own rights to Friary's Dor. I shall lose it if I don't."

He listened, walking along beside me. I noticed that we were walking away from the village. After a moment he said: "And who is the man?" His voice was strangely rough and deep.

"Lord Quiller's nephew. They own the castle."

"I see. Do you—have you met this nephew?"

I shook my head. "No. I've never met him, but—" I stopped, biting my lip, recalling Father's advice.

"You were saying?" he prompted. He stopped and turned to face me. We had left the village behind and were now on the cliff path. The sunlight gleamed on his black hair, and I thought how truly handsome he was.

"Oh. It was nothing. Just something my father told me." How close he was, and every pulse in my body quickened and caused my blood to tingle. "Your arm. Has it healed?" I looked up into those eyes.

"Yes, thanks to you," he said.

"No stiffness when you move?"

"None whatsoever." He moved his arm to show me. "I'd say your grandfather taught you well."

Again we were silent and strolled along, aware of each other.

He said: "When does this marriage take place?"

Perhaps he was calculating; it occurred to me that his business just might be *The Dark Lady*, and if it were, he might not be so free to sail into the cove as he'd like to. But I knew the ship was not in the cove to-day.

"I heard Father mention New Year's," I said, rather disinterestedly.

"Ah, so soon, then?" He lifted those magnificent brows. "He is fortunate, you know, this Lord Quiller's nephew." I felt the color rise to my cheeks.

"Maybe he is, but I'm not," I retorted, remembering the woman I'd seen in the book shop.

"You can refuse," he said.

"No. I can't refuse—I won't because I love my home here. I gave my word to my father. I won't go back on that now."

We walked on slowly. He was wearing a dark blue frock coat that looked well on him. I was drawn to him and couldn't deny it even to myself.

"No. I'm sure you wouldn't go back on your word to anyone," he said. "And somehow I do believe you haven't mentioned what transpired between us that night. Am I right?" He smiled down into my eyes. How cruel the world was, I thought suddenly, for fate to mismatch people. Why couldn't it have been this man instead of someone I could never like?

"No. I have said nothing."

"Then I was right about you." He reached for my hand and kissed it gallantly.

My blood tingled. "I—I don't even know who you are," I said quickly, trying to hide my emotions. "Are you the captain of *The Dark Lady?*" A flicker of surprise glinted in his eyes.

"You saw *The Dark Lady?*" He was cautious.

"Yes. She was anchored in Friars Cove the night I came home from London. And," I made a wild guess, "last night I watched her sail into the cove. Are you her captain?"

He still held my hand in his; I felt it tighten, and for a second I knew a tingle of fear touch my heart. What might he not do to one who knew so much?

"So you have detected my secret, Miss Dillard. That could be very dangerous for you, you know. Especially if you . . ."

"If I told my father, you mean?"

A smile played around the corners of his mouth. "In

a sense. But I should be flattered that you haven't found it necessary to mention what you have seen."

I laughed. "No. It's true. I haven't."

"I cannot help but wonder why you have not." He let my hand go.

"I don't know the answer to that," I said slowly. "But tell me, are you dealing in smuggling?"

His eyes were on my face again, searching, measuring. "But you are perceptive, Miss Dillard. I should have thought as a member of the delicate sex you would have gone into a panic with even the thought; you do not. I am amazed."

"Well. Are you?" I asked.

"Am I what?"

"A smuggler as well as the captain of *The Dark Lady?*"

"There are some things best left unsaid, Miss Dillard," he said, choosing his words carefully. "I have a request to ask of you. Will you have dinner with me aboard my ship tonight?"

The question took me off guard, and I could only stare at him.

In my hesitation he said: "Let me repay you for the kindness you have shown me on our previous meeting. That is why I came back, to thank you properly. You saved my arm, if not my life, that night. I can think of one way in which to show my gratitude. And that is for you to accept my invitation to come aboard *The Dark Lady.*"

"*The Dark Lady* isn't in Friars Cove," I said. "Where is she?"

That secret laughter was in his eyes again. "I sailed her up the coast, not wanting to take chances with your father being there. Tonight she will be in Friars

Cove. You will come, won't you?"

I couldn't answer because I was stricken with a new flame that coursed through my blood and quite fearful that he would read it in my eyes or my voice. I had to look out at the sea, but I knew he was not deceived.

"You will come, won't you? Let's make the most of what we have." His voice was low, and I was conscious of what my own heart was telling me.

"Yes. I will come." My voice quivered slightly. "What time shall I come?"

"I'll come for you; be at the tower at ten o'clock. The servants should be asleep by then. You will not be afraid?"

I shook my head. "No. I'm not afraid."

"Tonight, then, at ten o'clock by the tower."

"Whom shall I know is escorting me?" I knew my question was coy, and I saw amusement light his eyes.

"You can say Captain Dark will be escorting you to dine on *The Dark Lady,*" and he bowed gallantly over my hand. Then he left me at the bend in the path where it forked three ways and watched me as I took the one that led directly to the house.

I had hardly entered the house when Grace came looking for me. "Oh, there you are," she said excitedly. "Meg said she saw you enter the back way. Your trousseau came just after you left, Honor. And I might say, Mrs. Barrows and I have been in stitches over the finery of such a wardrobe of clothes! We laid them out for you because I didn't think you'd mind."

"Oh, but I'm glad you did," I said anxiously, with a sudden joy of knowing I would have something nice to wear tonight for my very secret rendezvous with Captain Dark! No surge of guilt bothered me that these clothes were to be used as my wedding clothes with another man. I wanted to look nice for the man I was meeting tonight.

Grace and I went up the stairs into my room. I was awed, too, at the soft velvets of lemon and tangerine gowns; the lilac and blue silks embroidered with spangles; fine gauzy muslins from India and France in the purest shades of white and gray and blue. There were ribbons in rainbow shades, dainty lace underwear and stockings, not to mention the cloaks and velvet slippers and soft leather buskins worn only by the gentlest of genteel ladies.

A short time later I bathed and then informed Grace that I would retire early for bed, as I was feeling a little exhaustion from the walk in the village. It was simple in the end, and I was left alone.

At nine I heard the stable clock strike the hour, and I carefully began to dress in the lilac silk that had caught my fancy. I left my hair unbound and tied it with a purple velvet ribbon; I flattered myself into thinking he would notice what I wore.

When I was sure the house had settled down and the servants were in their rooms, I crept down the stairs to my grandfather's study and heard the clock strike ten as I let myself out the door. The moon was already up in the sky, a pale nocturn glow that sharpened the shadows. As I left the cloisters, I thought of the man I'd seen last night. Had he warned Captain Dark of my father's presence? Perhaps I would find the answer tonight.

CHAPTER SIX

HE reached out from the shadows and took my arm; I knew a moment of panic, but when I was drawn close to him, seeing the flash of his smile, I felt at ease.

"You came. I thought you might back out at the last minute."

"I gave you my word. How could I back out, Captain Dark?"

He pulled my hand through his arm, and we descended the path to the cove. "Ah, but ladies have been known to change their minds. But you have come, and with no qualms or conscience toward the man you are to marry?"

A sense of recklessness washed over me. The picture of that woman in the book shop rose in front of me, and I was suddenly angry. Well, why couldn't I have my own past, too, as Father suggested I had? If I were caught, I might be branded as a brazen, shameless creature, but I didn't care.

He was searching my face intently, and I wondered how much he was seeing there. "You are angry. It shows clearly, you know, by the set of your mouth and that defiant look in your eyes. Are you wishing you had not come?"

I laughed. "On the contrary, I am very glad I did

come. I wouldn't miss this experience for the world!"

"Then I'm very happy I suggested it." He caught my mood as we walked quickly down the path. The moonlight touched his face. He had dressed for the occassion, too, I saw, and in the light from the lantern on the pier I glimpsed the mulberry coat and light tan breeches, his shirt frilled with lace at the collar and wrists. He seemed more like the cavalier—dashing, bold, and very daring. I knew I would not regret this night.

The Dark Lady was anchored a little way out, and Captain Dark helped me descend into the small boat alongside the pier, then climbed down after me. Two lanterns glowed in the night from the deck of the silent ship, and we both were silent as he rowed us to the side. I was helped up the ladder and assisted onto the deck by a huge black Nubian who had a gold earring dangling from one ear, a bright red and gold turban wrapped around his head. He grinned as I blinked my surprise and remembered suddenly what I'd heard about Captain Dark. I furtively glanced around me, guessing that I'd heard right and that the man was indeed what they said he was and more. But no other person was in sight.

My host came up behind me and swung himself easily down to the deck. It was a deck with no signs of disorder about it and had a shining look of a man-of-war.

"This is Abdullah, Miss Dillard. He is the most important member of my crew, as you will witness very soon. Abdullah, this is my lady, Miss Dillard, our guest this evening."

Grinning broadly, Abdullah bowed deeply from the waist, his great black eyes upon my face. He didn't speak, however, only grinned, and his skin shone like black satin.

"Abdullah is our chef," Captain Dark said, "and our dinner is waiting. Let's sample it. Come along." He laughed lightly and led me through a swinging door and down some steps through a galley and into a dark, richly paneled room.

There was a polished table with a bowl of red roses in the center and two places set for dinner. "My cabin," he said, closing the door behind us.

I glanced around me, surprised that it could be so restful. He was watching me. "You like it?" he asked.

"Yes," I answered, allowing him to take my cloak. I saw his eyes move over my gown appreciatively, and I was pleased that I had chosen to wear it. But he said nothing, and I gazed about me again.

It was a man's room—strong and dark like the man who pulled out the chair from the table for me. Silver gleamed on the fresh linen cloth beside the pewter plates and cups. I imagined the roses had been a last-minute arrangement, and it occurred to me they might have come from Peacock's own greenhouse.

"So this is where you live," I said, appraisingly. "Yes, I like it. I had no idea—"

"That I was a man of good taste, Miss Dillard?" He raised his brows slightly. "I'm surprised at you. As you can see for yourself, I enjoy privacy, too. My crew is on skeleton staff for a few hours, so that's why you saw only Abdullah. We are very organized."

It was almost a luxurious room, I thought, as a silence fell between us. Then I said: "Why are you a smuggler?"

He sat down opposite me. "There are no real dark reasons why," he answered. "I'm hired to do a job for the merchants who find it hard to get their exports out to France and Italy. I have my share of satisfaction in seeing it gets done with minimum bloodshed. It offers an escape, if you like, from the ordinary humdrum of life."

"I think I can understand that," I said slowly.

"Do you, Miss Dillard? Do you really understand?" That glimmer of amusement in those eyes was familiar to me now.

"Yes."

"But you are puzzled, aren't you? Because your father is so adament against it."

It was my turn to be surprised. "How did you know about my father? Do you know him?"

"No. I've not met him formally. But I do know of him. He is very brave, and who hasn't heard of Sir Arthur Wellesley's 52nd Regiment in Portugal? A great general, I believe, with such patriots like Colonel Dillard to back him up."

I nodded, feeling foolish and knowing how a sense of distrust could easily come to one who indulged in spying as I had done.

At a knock on the door, my host called "Enter," and Abdullah came in bearing a large tray with covered dishes on it that he carefully placed on a sideboard near us. He proceeded to fill our plates with lobster, prepared in the French way, with a hot butter sauce brushed lightly over the delicacy and broiled to a golden turn and a green salad with herbs, oil, and lemon. On the sideboard there was a plate of French pastries, cheese, and fruit. A slim bottle of wine was placed at the side of my host.

Abdullah didn't speak, which I thought odd. His face was pleasant, as if he took delight in serving us. I had seen several Nubian slaves in London town houses, but Abdullah seemed magnificent to me. I guessed it was because of his unique clothes; billowing bloomer-type pantaloons of creamy material with a scarlet sash, they could have come right out of the Arabian Nights. His shirt and jacket vest were no less fantastic in color, and he wore a round gold medallion on a long chain around his neck.

"Thank you, Abdullah," Captain Dark said when the Nubian hovered over the table after he'd served us. "That will be all for now, I think."

Abdullah smiled at me in his strange silent manner and left the room. I was aware my host was watching me intently.

"You are wondering about Abdullah," he said as he poured the wine into the thin crystal. "He is a Nubian, a former slave. I found him in Madagascar where he was living after he'd escaped from his master. He doesn't talk because his master had his tongue cut out when he was a youth. His master was a pirate. I took Abdullah with me, and although he is free, he is devoted to me. I owe my life several times over to him."

I don't know why I believed him, but I did. In the silence that followed the strains of someone plucking on a lute somewhere fell softly in the room about us. It was a haunting melody, quite appropriate to the mood and soft candlelight around us. I glanced at my companion's face and marveled that his life—so fantastic—should touch mine and that I was sitting here in the intimacy of his cabin, knowing that all too soon I would never see him again. I couldn't bear that thought and tried to forget it.

We ate our dinner; the meal was superb, the wine

sweet and cool. "Tell me about yourself," I said after a while. "Is your name truly Captain Dark?"

His uninhibited laugh rang in the room. "You are very inquisitive tonight. But no. It is a name I took when my family no longer claimed me as their son."

"You sound cynical. Did they disinherit you? Why?"

He shrugged his shoulders. "I couldn't conform to their . . . shall we say, shallow ideal of what an obedient son should be. I left home early, my father giving me my portion of inheritance, and like the prodigal, I am living my own life in a far country. I built *The Dark Lady*, and after a few years of privateering in the Spanish Americas, I came back to fair England, to be hired by our loyal merchants to fight the unfair revenues. My father sits in the seat of High Peers, organizing those burdensome revenues."

"You are opposing your father, then, by smuggling illicit merchandise."

He inclined his head. "If you like. I call it helping the people who are most affected by this economy tie-up."

"But it is against the law, isn't it?"

" 'Render unto Caesar.' They are bad laws, and this is one sure way to remedy them in the end. Can you understand that, Miss Dillard?"

"Of course. I can understand that the little man in-between war and the high taxes is always the one to be crushed. And you want to help them."

"Of course."

"Do you find your life happy?" I asked as he cut a chunk of cheese and passed it to me on the plate.

"I am content," he said as he reached out and took a tobacco jar down from a closed cabinet behind him. He asked politely if I minded his smoking, and when I said, "No. Go ahead," he shook the mixture into his hand and filled the pipe, then lit it with the candle on the table.

"One day they will catch you."

He leaned back in his chair and looked at me with narrowed eyes. "Perhaps," and another silence stretched between us.

"What brought you to Friars Cove that night you were wounded? Who really shot you?"

Just watching the laughter play around his mouth and eyes gave me sheer pleasure; it made him seem boyish.

"You did not for one moment believe it was a hunting accident?" I shook my head. "I thought so. It was all right, I can assure you. Someone mistook me for someone else and took a shot at me. It was simply my misfortune to be there." He laughed. "For the past three years I have used Friars Cove as my refuge, and although I didn't use the house, I used the infirmary. It's been quite safe, with none of the servants about. The old butler and his wife moved down to the cottage, and the stableman and his wife were no bother. I was content."

"And Tom Pegnally at the winery?"

"Ah. Tom Pegnally and Moll are a great help."

I should have known, but I was dumfounded. So it was true after all. "Tom?" Moll had lied for him. It must have been Tom who warned Captain Dark last night, of course. How else would Tom get his cider and wine exported?

His eyes were laughing at me. "Tom is very resourceful; without him I couldn't use Friars Cove as a refuge."

"And what will you do when Heath Quiller moves

into the Dor?" I hated myself for asking, and I flushed warmly.

"By that time, perhaps . . ." He left off, and we were silent again while he smoked. I brooded upon the thoughts of the man I was being forced to marry. Would he care if his wife knew a smuggler, had dinner with him in the intimacy of a cabin like this? Would he talk to me as this man was doing? The vision of that woman I'd seen flashed across my mind, and I guessed that Heath Quiller would never truly see me as this man did.

Suddenly I said: "I overheard my father and Lord Quiller discuss you this morning, Captain Dark. You're known as 'the notorious Captain Dark, a smuggler who is getting away with murder.' I'm certain Lord Quiller is anxious to have you caught. Won't it be dangerous for you in the future if you use Friars Cove?"

He stared at me in a strange manner. "Would you truly care about the danger for me, Miss Dillard?" he asked softly. My heart turned over with ecstasy.

"I—I wouldn't want to see you . . . caught, my lord." My voice was barely audible.

He was silent so long that I thought he hadn't heard. But he said: "Then you could do me a great service, if you will."

"And what is that?" I watched as he stood up and went to open a drawer. He brought out a book, which he opened and placed on the table in front of me.

"I would like you to join my ship's company, to sign your name among the faithful. You will be the first and the last lady to do so." He smiled, reaching for his quill, dipped it in the inkwell, and handed it to me without another word.

I saw the written words *The Dark Lady* and underneath a list of names. Impulsively I signed my name on the page beneath the others, then handed it back to him. He took the pen and recorded the date: December 4, 1811.

"You are one of us now." "Whenever I bring my ship into this cove, I know I shall be received with welcome and without fear of the enemy. I'm sure we can outsmart Lord Quiller's nephew." He smiled, took my hand in his, and pulled me to my feet.

"You must go back to the house now or you will be missed. But one day you must allow me to take you along when we sail. Would you like that?"

I was excited. "I should love it," I said. "But—" I frowned as he helped me into my cloak. "Will you be staying here for long?"

"I expect to be here for at least another three weeks or more before I sail. Will you give me some information?"

"Of what sort?" I asked as we left the room and went on deck.

"Will there be many visitors to Friary's Dor?"

I glanced up at him. "You're concerned that someone just might come upon you unaware? Don't worry," I laughed. "There won't be visitors, especially my father, I'm certain of that. His new bride is quite frightened of isolated country houses. Father was glad to get his assignment at the Margate Garrison." I told him this as a matter of course so that he would know about it.

He helped me down the ladder into the small boat and came after me. He said: "Then we shall see each other and often."

I caught my breath, for it hurt suddenly to breathe.

"You must know we cannot—I cannot! It wouldn't be fair to you, nor to myself." I whispered.

"You are one of my ship's company now, and the crew will want you to come aboard."

"I cannot," I said despairingly. "I'm to go into Margate very soon—tomorrow, I think, to make the final . . ." I couldn't continue, and I averted my eyes as we pulled up alongside the pier.

"Perhaps when you meet this Heath Quiller, you might find him a likable fellow."

"Likable, yes, to his mistress!" I cried out in anguish, an angry explosion inside me.

Surprised, he looked at me. "Mistress? You know of one?"

I glanced at him as he helped me from the boat. "One of many, I daresay! She was bold enough to come to Friarsgate asking for him and how she could get to the castle. I saw her today in the village book shop."

"You saw her? But how did you guess? Surely it *was* a guess? Perhaps you were mistaken. She could have been his sister or a cousin. What did she look like?"

He was being kind for my sake, and I appreciated his concern as he encouraged me to talk it out.

"She was more than beautiful, and I wonder what he will see in me after knowing her! That I can say she is exquisite is only because it's true. I won't deny it; red-gold curls and dark green eyes. It would turn any man's head."

"So that was why you were upset when I saw you!" he said. "But some men may not prefer red-gold curls and green eyes." His voice was soft and close to my ear as we began to walk up the path. "I'm sure that once this Heath Quiller sees you, he will prefer dark hair, long like yours with a ribbon and clear gray eyes,

to such a brazen creature as you paint Miss Exquisite,
gold hair and all." He was teasing me.

"Oh!" I exclaimed suddenly. His hand was warm on
my arm, and I thought he was going to take me in his
arms as he had that other night, but he did not. We
came to the tower, and although he still held my arm,
he did not pull me to him.

"I will see you again, Honor," he said in a low determined voice. "We shall dine together again in my
cabin. I'm sure of it. Now it is time for you to get back
to the house. Everything we've done must be kept ab-
solutely secret. You agree to this?"

He let go of my arm and stood from me. "Yes. I
agree," I whispered.

"Then, *au revoir*."

I turned and ran across the turf to the cloisters,
glancing back when I had reached them. He was still
there. When I let myself into the house and finally
reached my room, I went to the window and stared
out.

The white of his shirt frill was gleaming in the dark
shadow, and he left the tower and moved down the
path. So he knew which window to look for, I thought
happily, as I undressed and went to bed. He had seen
the movement of my body in the window without the
aid of a light.

CHAPTER SEVEN

It was a blustery day with a restless sky when Grace and I set out for Margate with Jason driving the carriage. Clouds scudded before the cold Channel winds, and gulls swooped in from the sea, which was as colorless as the day.

Grace and I sat in the carriage, a rug tucked around our legs; the plum-colored velvet gown and pelisse with the matching bonnet I wore were not sufficient to keep the cold out. Grace was in her second-best sarcenet gown and warm cloak, with an orange feather on the gray bonnet brim.

The prospect of meeting Heath Quiller was not a pleasant thought; I had many mixed emotions, knowing that it was the purpose of this journey to meet and then sign the final agreements.

Before us suddenly was Margate, a bustling seaport town with row upon row of Tudor cottages built right down to the waterfront. During the summer months it was a popular health resort, and I recalled that Lady Kitty Wellesley had spent the greater part of the summer with her children here on this coast and in Margate. Now soldiers and sailors thronged the streets.

There were always ships docked at the wharves along Fishersgate Lane and Gulls Walk, in from some

foreign port, until recently. The war prevented their
sailing, and the laggered trade resulted in devious
smuggling. The town was built for such lawlessness,
and I knew that Captain Dark must be acquainted
with some of those cellars under the waterfront.

It was a busy sight when we came into town; the
docks were loaded. It looked as if half of His Majesty's
navy was in the harbor; barks and barkentines; lug-
gers and brigs, frigates and sloops of war with their
gun heads covered, all were massed in the port, their
mizzen booms and bowsprits almost touching, their
webbing etched against the early-morning sky.

The house Father and Cecily lived in was on a hill-
side away from the port. A cold wind was whipping
around the corners when Grace and I stood at the door
to be admitted inside by the housemaid. She led us to
a charming parlor and took our wraps.

"Sir Reginald asked that you wait here," she said,
and left us to ourselves. The room was sunny and
warm, already reflecting Cecily's personality. Bowls of
fresh-cut flowers scented the room, and most of the
color was rose and gold. Beneath the gilt and white
furniture there were Indian and Turkish carpets, the
latest rage.

This must be Father's wedding gift to Cecily, I
thought. How different it was from Friary's Dor! In
the next moment the door opened, and Father came
in, dressed in his uniform. I was surprised to see him,
for I thought he would be at the garrison by this time.

"Ah, good morning, Grace. And Honor, my dear. I
see you came as I bid. Did you have a fair journey?"
He directed this question toward Grace, who curtsied
as was proper. "Oh yes, Sir Reginald, we did," she
said. "My, but it's brisk out, though. The wind is from

the Channel. Winter is upon us."

"Yes, so it is," Father remarked, his hands patiently clasped behind him. Then he said: "Grace, the maid will show you to yours and Jason's room. I hope you'll both be comfortable. I've ordered some refreshment to be brought up to you. I want to visit with my daughter before Lady Dillard arises."

"Very well, sir," Grace said affably. "I'd like that, and thank you kindly, sir. And, sir, am I to stay? I mean with Miss Honor until—" Her eyes were round and bright, uncertainty in them.

"By all means, Grace! She will need you, I think." He smiled not unkindly. "And I thank you for complying with my wishes."

"I was glad to, sir. You can count on me."

"I know that, Grace. I have, remember? Now. Here is Mrs. Larks. She will show you all you need."

I had stood by and watched this little by-play with almost a detached sense of being, and then Father asked me to come with him into his study down the hall. As he closed the door behind us, I said:

"I had no idea you'd be living off post, Father. The house is charming, and—Well, I'm surprised everything seems so settled for you here." I turned and smiled at him. "The house already reflects Cecily's charming personality. It's rather amazing."

That pleased him, I could see at once. "Do you think so, Honor? I've tried to please her, and she does love pretty things. It makes her bloom, if you know what I mean."

At this unusual small talk, I studied my father thoughtfully, then said: "Yes. I think I know what you're saying, and you've done well."

His study was a quiet room, with nothing feminine

about it. He moved to his desk with a gesture for me to be seated, and then he sat down, facing me. "I'm conducting my assignment from here. In other words this is my headquarters as well as our living quarters. Several members of my staff are billeted nearby, so it is easy, and the garrison is not far from here."

I knew he did not have me in his study to talk lightly; I guessed that what he had to say to me would not be easy, for he was deliberating. A maid knocked and entered with a tea tray, then left us.

After helping myself to a cup of hot tea and handing Father one, I said, "Father, please tell me what you have on your mind." I kept my voice light, but I gazed at him with defiance, and he saw that at once.

He was silent as he drank his tea, studying me through those vivid eyes; then he sighed heavily and placed the cup down. "Yes, you're right, of course. I'll come to the point." For one wild moment I had the thought that Heath Quiller had reneged on the arrangement. But Father said:

"Some plans have been changed. I had hoped the marriage would take place in the week after Christmas or New Year's. But for some reason Lord Quiller's nephew will be gone then, and he wishes to be married at once—tonight, in fact, after the reception here. This reception could not be avoided, unfortunately; it was planned, and it's too late to cancel now. However, it will be held early—at four this afternoon—and the wedding will be at eight-thirty, in Friarsgate Church of all places. I couldn't get him to change his mind. It was his wish, and I couldn't refuse him."

I felt myself pale. "Tonight! But Father! I simply can't!" A wild feeling of being trapped engulfed me. "How can you expect me—"

"Honor. Believe me. I couldn't see any valid reason not to go along with his request. You gave your word, and I assure you, the young man is sincere. Your wedding gown has arrived, and I must say, you do justice to that lovely gown you're wearing." He came to me and took both my hands in his while his eyes moved over my clothes.

I was struck dumb. But he said: "Everything is in order; the license and the formal paperwork has been taken care of, and you will sign that tonight at the church. The banns have been put up. Now you simply must pull yourself together and be logical about it."

"When do I meet—" I stopped and glanced up at him.

"When do you meet Heath Quiller? Sometime just before the reception, I believe. Sir Mark is coming with him, and Heath will form the line with us. Afterward —well. You must conduct yourself properly, my dear. I expect it of you. Now go to your room. Grace will help you do all the necessary things which should be done. Come along."

I couldn't feel anything; my brain seemed to stop working, and Father led me from the study and up the stairs to a second-floor room where the curtains were drawn back and the windows overlooked the town of Margate and the port. He stayed with me until Grace came in, then left me in her care.

Grace had the bright idea that my hair should be washed, and she ordered the hot water brought up. I allowed her to scrub it as I sat in the little dressing room before the fire. She rinsed it and toweled it dry, then began to comb it as she used to do when I was a child. I was wrapped in a soft warm robe, oblivious to her cheerful chatter.

I felt as if I had been given my sentence of doom; only one thing mattered to me now; I would never see my Captain Dark again, and tears came to my eyes unbidden.

It was about two-thirty when Cecily knocked and entered. My wedding gown was hanging in the wardrobe, the veil already pressed, but I hadn't the heart to admire it.

Cecily conferred with Grace in low, soft tones for a moment; then Grace left, leaving Cecily alone with me. She had brought a tray in with her, and now she placed it down on the small table between two chairs drawn up at the fire.

"Darling," she said softly. "Please do come and sit here with me. I shall need this refreshment, and I wanted to share it with you. You must have nourishment, for the evening will be long. Please do come."

I reluctantly sat down across from her. "There," she smiled. "It's far wiser to look after your health in strenuous times like this. Have some of this strong, hot tea, with cream and sugar." She poured it and handed the rose-bordered cup to me. Then she passed a plate of thinly sliced bread and butter. I helped myself, and when I took a swallow of the hot tea, I realized I hadn't eaten all day and was hungry.

Cecily was lovely in the blue robe with the lace falling away from her white arms. Her dark gold hair was done up in a topknot of shining curls, tied with a blue ribbon. I had forgotten just how beautiful she was. I guessed she had come to me when all others had failed to get a response, probably at Father's exasperation.

"Have you met him, Cecily?"

She looked up at me, her pink lips parting. "You

mean Mister Quiller? No, Honor. I haven't. He's coming this afternoon, I believe." She laughed suddenly. "But Reggie said he is good-looking and young enough for you. And of course, I trust Reggie's good judgment in matters of this nature. I'm sure—" She bit her lip prettily and stared at me. "Would you . . . do you want me to tell you anything? I mean, about getting married? Or have you been told?" Her eyes were wide, ready for confidences.

It was clear that she was sounding me out, that Father had sent her to prepare the blow, the great shocking truth of what I was to expect from the wedding night.

I smiled wanly. "I've been told, Cecily, of course. You can assure Father that I know about those things. But it was good of you to care. Thank you." My cheeks burned with some embarrassment, for her stare was oddly probing.

"Then why are you so seemingly unprepared? I thought you were aware of this arrangement. Most girls would consider themselves fortunate in having their future secured in such a manner." She was frowning slightly, her head tilted to one side.

She was chiding me gently, I knew. But she came as a friend as well as my father's wife. She was older than I by at least nine years and therefore wiser. I was behaving badly, quite like a child. It was my problem, one that I would have to face and live with, and I didn't want to burden anyone else with it. So I sighed resignedly and said:

"You're right of course. I'm behaving childishly. It's just that it was a shock to know it must take place and so soon. I hadn't gotten used to the idea of it all, and now this—and tonight. It's all rather sudden." I gestured with my hand to what I was feeling.

She set her cup down. "Yes, of course it was sudden. I was completely startled, too, when Reggie told me last evening. But you must remember this: If it must take place, the sooner the better to have it over. You'll see what I'm talking about."

It came to me that she was being kind for my sake, but I also knew that she had married my father because she had a choice and most likely loved him. It hadn't been arranged for her.

Suddenly she was gay. "Oh, I must tell you now. My cousin is coming for a visit and I believe she will be at the reception this afternoon. I do want you to meet her. But we must get you dressed now. May I dress your hair? You have such abundant tresses, and I would be delighted to arrange it for you!"

She was deft and very talented, and when she had completed it, I looked entirely different. She had cleverly arranged the crown of braids on top, with a large glossy curl falling down from the left side on my neck. "When we dress you for the wedding, I shall let your hair all the way down, with a smaller braided crown for the veil, but for now how do you like it?"

"Oh Cecily!" I said softly, staring at my reflection in the mirror. She had chosen a white Indian silk gown with seed-pearl embroidery around the hem and on the bodice for me to wear and had tied the scarlet satin ribbon into a large bow in back. "You've made me look different somehow, and I like it."

She stood back a pace to regard me. "You should be shown off as my husband's very lovely daughter, Honor. I'm certain he will be proud of you tonight. Now I must go dress if I'm to get down to the hall on time." She suddenly leaned over and kissed my cheek with her cool lips, and then she turned and ran from the room like a young girl.

She had barely gone when I was summoned to Father's study. As I entered the room, an elderly gentleman stood up from the chair he was in. I glanced around the room, but no one else was there except him and Father. I felt both relief and disappointment, knowing Heath Quiller was not yet here, as Father hurried across the room to me.

He introduced us. "Lord Quiller, Sir Mark—my daughter Honor."

Sir Mark was tall and quite portly. His florid face suggested he had trouble breathing. He had great dark eyes, white hair, and a thick, luxuriant mustache. The black frock coat and gray breeches were correct, as well as the black Hessian boots he wore.

He bowed slightly to me and smiled. "Miss Honor, I'm deeply pleased to meet you at last. And I can see that all I've been told of you is true and more." The black eyes were probing yet kind.

I wondered what he had heard and how he could know it was true when he didn't know me? But I murmured politely: "Thank you, Lord Quiller."

"Oh, you must call me Sir Mark, my dear. We're to be family, you know." He chuckled.

"Sir Mark it is, then." I said, curtsying slightly.

"Miss Honor, I want to express my gratitude to you for complying with these arrangements so hastily put together." We seated ourselves near the fire. "My nephew is most anxious to have the wedding tonight because after a honeymoon is over, he must travel to the Continent for a long stay. I deeply regret that my wife, Lady Catherine, is unable to be here to attend this reception and meet you formally. But she will be at the church for the wedding."

I couldn't think of anything to say to this, and Sir Mark continued:

"I must also apologize that my nephew sent word he will be a trifle late, unavoidably detained by an unforeseen urgent matter. But he did wish me to convey to you that he is anxious to meet you. He simply has not been here in England, and he arrived only three days ago. His work takes him out of the country for long periods."

I struggled with my pride in that moment, for I was tempted to speak my mind. So that was the way it was to be, I thought. He could go on his trips anywhere and stay as long as he wished. It was an uncomfortable moment, and I said nothing, not really accepting the formal apology for my bridegroom's behavior.

Sir Mark broke through my thoughts. ". . . he asked me to give you this, most unorthodox, I know, but one that seems fitting and necessary. It will seal a most delicate situation for all of us." He brought a ring from his pocket and showed it to me. The large ruby encircled with diamonds glowed in the room like a sanctuary lamp.

"Heath asked me to place it on your finger for him, in front of your father, my dear. Will you allow me?" The old man was smiling gently, and he took my hand and slipped the ring on the left finger. "This is a Quiller jewel, Honor. Wear it with pride and grace." He leaned over and touched my hand with his lips.

All I could manage was: "It's exquisite." That pleased him. A few minutes later I left the room, for Sir Mark seemed to tire, and Father went to fetch Cecily. It occurred to me that the old man was indeed worried that his nephew might not show up for the wedding.

CHAPTER EIGHT

I STARED down at the ring on my finger. Rubies were supposed to have some meaning, to bring health and happiness and wisdom. I wondered if fate had not been crossed somewhere, for truly how could I expect happiness in a marriage such as I was destined to now?

The guests began to arrive, and I stood with Father and Cecily in the receiving line. Heath had not shown up, and Sir Mark remained in the study. I was certain the old man was full of anxiety. How dare Heath exhibit such cruel behavior on such an important occasion! But I was angry, too, because it seemed more of a slap in my face; he didn't care enough to meet me before we joined our lives forever!

Cecily was a glowing enchantress beside Father. Her gown of sheer blue silk muslin trimmed with silver spangles, was like a cloud of softness around her. Around her cap of gold curls she wore a pearl tiara, and her laughter was as infectious as her personality.

It was then I received the shock of my life; through the door and with the guests who entered I glimpsed the young woman I'd seen in the Friarsgate book shop several days before. I could think only one thought then: *He* had the audacity to invite her! Of all the despicable . . .

Cecily burst out: "Marceline! But how glad I am that you could come after all!" She embraced the young woman fondly.

The woman laughed, her voice quite different from the impatient one in the book shop. "I wouldn't have missed it for the world, *ma petite cherie!*" I wondered if I could have been mistaken? "Oh, Marceline. This is my husband Sir Reginald and his lovely daughter Honor. Please be nice to them, darling, for they mean everything to me—my family now!" Her voice had a lilt in it.

"But of course, *cherie,*" Marceline said. "How do you do, Sir Reginald? Hon-or?" She arched an eyebrow at each of us, the long green eyes shaded by curling lashes. I hadn't been mistaken, and her accent was strong.

"This is my cousin, Marceline Bonet. I mentioned that she was in town," Cecily said to Reggie, "but darling, she has refused to stay with us. You must persuade her to change her mind, won't you?"

"Of course we shall," Father said magnanimously, which did surprise me. "Miss Bonet. You must consider this your home while you're in England. I won't take no for an answer, I warn you." He was charming.

Marceline allowed her eyes to rest on Father's smiling face. I caught a calculating gleam in those eyes, and I was disturbed more than ever.

A short time later music from the hall struck up, and Father and Cecily opened the dance with a lively waltz. Heath Quiller had still not come, and it seemed to create an uncertainty for Father, for me, and for Sir Mark, whom I noticed had come to stand inside the ballroom.

I gazed over the uniformed guests and lovely

gowned ladies, but there was no one whose face was
familiar. My glance rested momentarily on Marceline
Bonet; she wasn't lacking partners for the first waltz.
She would turn anyone's head, with hair like living
gold and that filmy Nile-green gown floating about
her! Something like envy stirred inside me as I watched
her.

Suddenly my arm was caught from behind and I
was spun about.

"Honor!" I was startled, then stunned, as the sea-
green eyes of Anthony Cordell, captain in the Dragoon
Guards, stared at me, my face, my neck, and over my
gown. I couldn't mistake that look, and it was far too
possessive.

"So it's you. Honor Dillard, Sir Reginald's lovely
daughter. I never thought to see you again. I didn't
know where you had gone; you ran off with no word,
and here you are in my superior's house! Why didn't
you let me know, Honor?"

"Let you know what, Anthony?" I said, laughing up
at him.

"That you were here in Margate with your father?
Why on earth didn't you tell me Colonel Dillard was
your father?" He laughed, too.

"How could I know you knew Colonel Dillard?"

We both laughed then. "To think that I'm his aide-
de-camp, and you're his daughter! It's almost too good
to be true. But I've found you at last. I've been frantic
to get in touch with you, darling. Let's get out of here.
Where can we go to talk?" He glanced around us.

I stared at him. "We have nothing to say to each
other, Anthony. I didn't run away, I came home for
good. I left London because I was tired of playing
those childish games with you. But how on earth did

you get assigned to my father's staff?"

His eyes were wide with questions; handsome Anthony Cordell. He would thrill some girls, but I looked on him as an undesirable acquaintance now, though it hadn't always been like that. His thatch of dark gold hair, cut short and curled slightly rather like a Roman, with neatly trimmed sideburns and a strong jawline, was like an aureate above the smooth tanned face. He was good-looking in the scarlet and gold dress uniform.

"Let's go somewhere to talk, Honor," he said, ignoring what I had just said to him. "It's much too noisy in here, and I have something I want to say to you." His hand was tight on my arm, and he would have led me from the room if Sir Mark had not prevented it by his sudden appearance at our side.

"Good evening, Captain Cordell. It is Anthony Cordell, is it not?" He stood taller than Anthony by several inches, reminding me of a great bird of prey.

Anthony's face darkened with a flush of anger. "Yes, Sir Mark. I'm Anthony Cordell."

The old man smiled. "You know Miss Dillard?"

"Yes, and very well," he answered curtly.

"We're friends, after a fashion, Sir Mark," I hastened to say before Anthony could say otherwise.

"Hm-mm, I see." A glimmer of amusement touched Sir Mark's mouth. "Are you aware that Heath, my nephew, is betrothed to Miss Dillard, Captain? Yes. They are to be married this night. I thought you might like to know about this. To pass it along to Sir Percival since Heath would not allow me to. You will be seeing Sir Percival sometime soon?"

Anthony glowered darkly and turned to me. "Is this true, Honor? Are you to be married to Heath Quiller?" He almost shook it out of me.

I stepped back a pace, not liking what I saw in his eyes. "Yes. It's true. We are to be married tonight." I lowered my eyes. I had no intention of explaining anything to Anthony. He wasn't entitled to an explanation, but I felt my face stain with color.

Sir Mark said dryly: "You both will excuse me now, I'm sure. Why don't you take Miss Dillard on the floor, Captain? After tonight, she will be the next Lady Quiller." The old man seemed to be gloating, and it puzzled me. He bowed slightly and left us.

Suddenly Anthony swept me onto the dance floor, his face a study in anger and humiliation.

He said: "Why did you do it, Honor? Why didn't you tell me that you knew Heath Quiller and that you were going to marry him?"

I couldn't answer him. His eyes blazed down into mine. "Why? For God's sake, why are you doing this? Is it because he can give you a title—something I couldn't give you? So he wins again! He always wins, and because of his . . . background! The almighty class distinction of birth between the noblesse and the working class! My God! And now he's claimed you, too!" His jaw hardened.

"I had no idea you were acquainted with the Quillers, Anthony. Do you know them well?"

"I should. They're my wealthy relations, and it galls me if you want to know the truth. Heath was a scoundrel from the cradle. We were always rivals in something. His conduct in and out of school was outrageous! He scorned everyone, including Sir Percival, and because he was a 'second' son of a good family, he could get away with it! My God! How I used to despise him for his lack of morals!"

"Sir Percival? Then he is—"

"Sir Percival is Heath's father. Heath was disowned time and time again. I thought you knew Lord Quiller, Sir Percival, that is." He kept his eyes on my face, searching, reading what was there.

"No. I don't know Sir Percival. I've met only Sir Mark Quiller," I said slowly, remembering again what my father had told me of Heath's being Sir Mark's heir. "So you are a relation to Heath?"

"Unfortunately." His voice was rough. "But Sir Percival was and still is a kind and rather noble man. He gave me a chance in life, Honor. You see, my family was poor. He sent me to the military school, and he bought my captaincy. I owe him my gratitude and loyalty. Lady Ernestina, his wife, is also very kind. Heath would even scorn *her!*"

"You are fortunate, then," I said.

I had never seen him so angry. "My God! Let's get out of here!" he whispered, and danced me over to the doors that led into the dim-lighted solarium, which was now deserted.

He placed his hands on my shoulders, gripping them. "You're being forced into this farce of a marriage, aren't you? That's why, isn't it?"

I had no words at that moment. He went on: "I love you, Honor," he whispered. "You knew that, yet you refused me last April. You knew then about Heath, and you didn't tell me about it. But I love you. He could never love you the way I do!" He pulled me to him roughly and kissed my lips possessively. I turned my face and moved out of his grasp.

"No! You must not. Don't ever do that again! I don't, I didn't know—" I put my hand up to my mouth.

In the silence that followed he stared hard at me. "I can't believe you would choose him so willingly,

Honor. Not Heath Quiller. He's not for you. And, by God, you're not to be his!" He reached out to me again, gripping my wrist.

"Let her go, Captain." A voice of steel broke in behind us. We broke apart guiltily and stared at the man who stepped out of the shadows.

For one mad second I was stunned. My heart dipped crazily, then began to race wildly. It was Captain Dark!

Anthony's hand tightened on my wrist as I tried to pull away. The two men measured each other across that small space, their eyes blazing.

"You didn't hear me correctly, Captain Cordell. I said, let her go." Again, that steel-like voice cut in that silence, and I felt Anthony's grip loosen my hand suddenly.

Anthony's voice was bitter: "You have your nerve, Heath. Do you imagine for one second that I'm going to stand by and allow you to take my girl for your wife?"

Had Anthony gone mad? For a moment I stared at both men.

"That's enough, Captain!" The words were cold and commanding. "This lady is my betrothed. We are being married tonight. I intend to see that you do not seek her company in the future." He turned to me. "Honor, I haven't had my dance with you; come along." And before I knew how it happened, his hand was firmly on my arm, and I was drawn close to his side.

He led me back into the gaily lighted room, placed his hand on my waist, and swept me out onto the dance floor. As I stared up into his face, I was stunned beyond my wits. By some devious trick I had been utterly made the fool by this man. Captain Dark was none other than Heath Quiller!

He was looking down at me, amused. "You didn't tell me you had a suitor, Honor. And so forceful a one."

That brought me to reality. "Your secret life is surfacing, too, my lord," I said testily. "Is it Captain Dark, or is it Heath Quiller?"

He raised those magnificent brows. "I wanted very much to explain to you several times, Honor. Please believe that. But you had such a vehement aversion toward Heath. Does it make a difference, knowing the truth?"

I was at a loss for words; a hot flush stained my cheeks, and I tried to concentrate then on the complicated steps of the waltz. He was a good dancer, and I floated around the room with him as if I were on air. We didn't talk after that, and when the dance ended, Heath led me over to where Father stood with Sir Mark.

"So you both have met." Sir Mark said jovially. "Very good."

"Yes. We've met, Uncle Mark," Heath kept his voice low. "But now, Sir Reginald, I do think it's time we start for the church. The weather outside is changing, and we don't want to be delayed by a storm."

As if in a daze, I allowed myself to bend at will, and I was whisked upstairs to my room, with Grace and Cecily attending me.

The gown was of the purest white satin covered with tulle and ornamented with row upon row of tiny scalloped lace frills. The bodice fit snugly, had a low decolleté neckline, and was embroidered with seed pearls. The long sleeves, puffed at the shoulders, were of transparent and delicate lace.

Cecily arranged my hair under the Chantilly lace veil. When she completed it, Father surprised me by coming in, and Cecily left us together. I was dimly aware of Grace moving about in the dressing room.

Father stared at me. "How lovely you are, Honor!" He kissed my cheek warmly, then brought out a box from his jacket and opened it. Inside was a large pearl pendant on a tiny gold chain and two small pearl droplet earrings. "Please accept these; they were your mother's. She wanted you to have them on your wedding day."

My throat suddenly constricted oddly. "Mother's." I didn't go on, and he said: "Let me help you with them." His hands were gentle and deft as he hooked the necklace around my neck; I fastened the earrings on, glancing into the mirror as I did so.

He stepped back to regard me. "You're every bit as lovely as your mother was, Honor. You have eyes like hers, you know, so clear a gray. She would have been proud of you this day. I am."

"Thank you, Father." My voice was a whisper.

"If you're ready, we'd better start. He helped me into the white velvet-lined cloak, and we descended the stairs, my arm through his.

I saw a sea of faces staring at me; the guests were lined up to watch me as I walked out to the waiting carriage. In those faces there were two I knew; Anthony, who hovered on the edge, his expression dark with anger, and the sylphlike creature in pale green, Marceline Bonet. Her face was white, and her eyes seemed too large in her face. There was shock, but something else, too, I recognized; hate, and it was directed at me.

The guests were waiting at the church in Friarsgate when our carriage pulled up in front of the stone steps. It was bitterly cold out, and the wind was wild, whipping around the corners in galelike strength. As I stepped inside the chancery, I pulled the veil down over my face, and the strains of the organ swelled out.

Then the doors opened, and I was walking down the aisle on Father's arm toward the altar; the glow of the sanctuary lamps were as red as the ruby on my finger. I felt like a different person, detached, seeing myself as from a distance.

I saw Cecily's lovely face; Grace was there, too, as were Dust and Mrs. Barrows. There were others, but I didn't recognize them. Anthony I did not see. And then I was at the altar, surprised that I could feel so detached and calm as I glanced up and met the eyes of the man I was to wed.

I reached his side, knowing those dark eyes were studying me carefully. He reached out with his big warm hand and took my cold one. He didn't smile; he seemed almost to frown in consternation as we turned to face the rector.

CHAPTER NINE

THE rector's voice boomed out. A dreamlike spell descended over me. I stood there, pale yet calm at Heath's side and heard my own voice clear and unhurried with the responses while allowing my fingers to pass from the Rector's thin hand into the bridegroom's keeping. Still in that spell, I heard Heath say:

"I, Heath Alexander Quiller, take thee, Honor Dillard, to be my wedded wife, to have and to hold from this day forward, for better, for worse, for richer for poorer, in sickness and in health, to love and to cherish till death us do part, according to God's Holy Ordinance; and thereto I plight thee my troth."

He spoke firmly and audibly but with an unemotional voice. I knew I shivered because of his tone, yet it was not I who did so but some woman who bore my name and spoke with my voice, who had for the moment, ceased to feel any emotion.

Heath took my hand and slipped the gold wedding band on my third finger next to the glowing ruby. The service ended, and Heath turned to me, lifted the lace veil, and kissed my mouth briefly with a cool passionless kiss. The organ burst into the "Wedding March," and we turned to be led to sign the register.

Sir Court Gannon had stood beside Heath throughout the service, and now he shook my hand and wished us happiness. I could only smile a frozen smile and thank him. Later, I learned he was Heath's best friend, the only one to come to our wedding. A mist of unreality lingered with me as we stood there; Father kissed me and shook Heath's hand, Cecily congratulated us, and Grace had tears in her eyes. Sir Mark and Lady Catherine wished us both happiness, and then it was over.

I was helped into the waiting carriage, and Heath sat down beside me. The door closed, and we were alone together in the dark of night. I heard the driver of the coach start up the horses, and we were off, to what destination I didn't know.

A warm rug was tucked around my lap and feet because it was very cold; but I felt neither the cold nor warmth as we sat in the silence together. Once I glanced up at him from the corner of my eye and had the impression he was holding a tremendous fury in check.

"How long have you known Anthony Cordell, Honor?"

"Oh, less than two years, I should think," I answered stiffly.

For a moment he said nothing, and I thought he put it from his mind, but he said: "From this hour I do not want you to receive him or be seen in his company. Do I make myself clear?"

I was appalled by the anger in his manner. His face was hard and cold, and his eyes so dark that I scarcely recognized him.

"I should think you would be the last one to make such a ridiculous demand, if you please, my lord," I said hotly. "How dare you—"

He cut in: "I'm warning you, Honor. You're my wife, and I do have that right to choose and to regulate your companions. Anthony Cordell is not to come near you again." He spoke slowly, deliberately, still keeping in check a great force of anger.

"And *your* companions, my lord?" I could hardly speak. "Are they not to be *regulated?* If I seem forward, it's only because I don't like the company you have been keeping, and I refer to a *Mademoiselle Bonet*, a recent companion of yours!"

His glance seemed to smoulder. "Ah yes. I seem to recall you mentioned someone like her—'exquisite,' you called her." He laughed, and my cheeks flamed as a hot tide of embarrassment swept over me. I was aware of his scrutiny, and I averted my own eyes for the moment.

His voice was level: "Just remember that I have given you fair warning, Honor. I'll not answer for what happens if I ever see him around you."

I laughed. "Your jealousy is unbecoming as well as unwarranted, my lord. I'll see my friends any time I choose."

He studied me for some time, rather darkly, but I could not read his thoughts. Then he said quietly, as if there had been no words between us: "My name is Heath, Honor. I would like you to call me by that, not 'my lord.' I ask it as a favor."

When at last the driver pulled to a stop in a cobblestone courtyard, I glanced out of the window into darkness, seeing nothing. The door opened, and Heath stepped out and helped me down.

"We'll be staying here for the night," he said. I looked up and saw the Three Friars Inn sign swinging overhead in the wind. Why had he chosen this, I wondered, as we hurried inside. The inn was on a lonely and isolated cliff overlooking the Channel; a stopping place for the stagecoaches from London and Canterbury to Dover, and three miles from Friary's Dor down the coast.

Heath led me inside, saying, "There's no private parlor, but since we are the only guests, we should be comfortable."

A fire burned on the hearth, and the smells of bread, roasting meat, and hot coffee lingered in the air. We were met by the landlord, a fact that betrayed all this had been planned in advance.

I went up to the room reserved for us where my lighter portmanteau was placed. The room was small but clean and fresh, and I was glad to escape Heath's presence. I drew the shutters, removed my cloak, and changed the wedding gown for something more suitable.

It was when I started to return downstairs that I opened the door to the narrow corridor and saw the open door of another room down the hall. Heath came out of that door, and behind him I glimpsed the person to whom he was talking.

Marceline Bonet stood outlined by the light. Her voice was low and stricken with anguish. "Heath! I didn't know you were getting married! I had no idea—"

"Yes you did, Marceline." His voice was harsh but low. "You knew it. What's more, you went to the castle and learned the truth from my Aunt Catherine! I warned you to stay away from there. Why did you go?"

"Where else should I have gone? To *Friary's Dor?*"

"Just you keep away from there, Marceline! And why did you follow me *here*, of all places?" I heard the incredulity in his cold voice.

"You know the answer to that as well as I do. I love you. I can't bear to see you married to *her!* Or to anyone but me!" She reached out to him.

I closed the door and found myself trembling with rage. A new feeling burst inside me, and I knew it for the jealousy it was. I was indignant and humiliated. How dare he have the audacity!

I bolted the door, brought out my warmest cloak, and took a swift look out the window. I had decided my course. Cautiously, I lifted myself over the casement and closed the diamond-paned window after me, then lowered myself off the flat roof and dropped to the ground some five or six feet below without mishap.

After a moment's hesitation I peeped into the window nearest me. It was the kitchen. Several people stood about: maids in their mobcaps and two grooms, laughing and talking. I didn't wait to see more, but ran to the back of the garden and crept along the hedgerow, keeping down so that I shouldn't be discovered.

The wind swept its fury at the hem of my cloak and gown, and it was difficult walking, fighting it and the darkness. But I knew that once I reached the path toward the cliffs, I could rest my mind. Hardly anyone knew this lonely stretch of coast, so I would not be discovered.

When I reached the path that led toward the chalk cliffs, I made a sharp turn to the right and went past Peacock's small cottage. It was dark, and I supposed they had gone to bed, for it was late. It was very cold by now, and a moist flake hit my face. There was only one light at the back of the house, and that was in Dust and Mrs. Barrow's room. I didn't take a chance on going into the house, rather, I slipped into the infirmary and closed the door carefully behind me.

In a short while I had a fire on the hearth and stretched my cold hands out to its warmth. I curled up in a chair, knowing in a little while I would rouse myself and make some fresh tea. But for now I was chilled, exhausted, and wretched.

Somewhere in the distance I heard the baying of one of Tom's hounds. It was a lost and forlorn sound, and I suddenly felt devastated. A sob bubbled up in my throat, and I let the tears spill down my cheeks unchecked. I gave myself to those tears, and all the self-pity and disappointments came to surface. What was going to be my fate now? A runaway bride . . .

So emerged into this self-pity, I didn't hear the door when it opened; I felt only the cold draft of wind, and I half-rose to my feet as fear pricked my heart.

Heath stood there, the door closed behind him, not moving. A sinister figure with the beaver hat cocked slightly, he was wearing a greatcoat I hadn't seen before. Our eyes met across that small distance, and I was afraid.

"Come here!" The order was sharp, abrupt.

My body began to tremble violently, and I knew my face was stained with tears; a sob escaped my throat. The firelight illuminated his face clearly, flickering on his hard jawline. He removed his hat and coat, casting them aside with one movement.

"Come here!" he commanded again, and the tremor of his voice startled me. I could not have moved had I wanted to, which I did not. But even in that moment of fear, something stirred within me, and I stood facing him defiantly. There was half the width of the room between us, and he was going to make that first move, I told myself.

"I—I care not to, my lord," I said in a voice not my own. It took him three strides to cross that room and reach out for me with his hands, grasping my arms. So sudden was his movement that I lost my balance and fell against him, gasping in pain.

"Did you think you could escape me so easily, or that I would let you go?" He glowered at me, and I saw the torment in his eyes. "You are married to me now—you're my wife, and don't you ever forget that, not for an instant!"

"Your wife! Even when you bring along your mistress on your wedding night?" I flung back at him. "Never! I'm not your wife—just a fixture for you in name only! And thats' all I will ever be!"

He stared at me as if I'd gone mad. A fierce, biting fury raged within me, and I clenched my fists against his hands, which were now gripping my wrists. My hair had come loose from the hood of my cloak, and as I tried to get free, it swung loose about my body.

"Oh, is that so?" He pulled me to him with a strength that was like steel. "I'll teach you a lesson in proper behavior to your husband! And I promise to begin that lesson right now!"

"Don't touch me! Not after you have been with her!"

His eyes blazed at me in the darkness. "I'll touch you whenever I please, and I please to do so now." He pulled me to him as though he would pull me into his body, his arms holding me.

"Let me go!" I cried. "Let me go! I won't let you touch me tonight!"

He flung his head back and laughed that wild uninhibited laugh of his. "There is only one way to teach you that lesson," he said half under his breath. He pressed his mouth down on mine, angry and hot, holding me in such a grip that I feared for my bones.

"Let me go!" I was maddened. "If you touch me to-night, Heath, I will kill you!"

"You will? Try it!" He half-pushed, half-carried me into the other room and thrust me down on the bed that was set up for patients' use. He half-fell over me, pinning me to the bedding.

I fought him, trying to get free, but he used brute force to hold me. His mouth was on mine, kissing me wildly, bruising and hurting my lips. Somewhere in the struggle my cloak had fallen from me, and as I felt the hardness of his warm body, I knew I was no match for his strength.

I was helpless and near to fainting when I heard him say:

"Is this how Anthony Cordell kissed you? Like this?" His lips were on my throat, and with a sharp movement his fingers began to rip my flimsy gown. As he lifted his head to look at me, I saw his face; his expression was that of a man tormented beyond endurance.

He must have seen the terror on my face, for all of a sudden, he turned and stalked out of the room.

CHAPTER TEN

It was some time before Heath came back into the room. As he neared the bed, I shrank back.

"You needn't be frightened of me, Honor. I behaved depraved. It won't happen again. We'll work this out whenever you are ready." His voice was calm and low, but decisive.

I stood up from the bed and clutched at my torn gown, my hair streaming about me in disarray. He brought my cloak to me and helped me into it. "I'll take you up to the house. You'll be more comfortable, I think." He didn't smile, but he was gentle.

He placed his hat on his head and put on the greatcoat; then he opened the door for me, and we went out into the night.

It was to my grandfather's rooms that Heath took me; I stared around me, bewildered. A warm fire glowed in the grate, and the large fourposter was made up with the coverlet folded back, the dark red curtains tied up.

Heath saw the expression. "I thought you'd be more comfortable in here since your old room has been rather dismantled. You don't mind, do you?" He lifted his eyebrows.

"No. It's all right, I don't mind."

He placed his hands on my shoulders and looked at me. "Honor, don't be afraid. Not of me. In the morning your trunks will be here. For now, go to bed and sleep. Goodnight." He bent and kissed my lips very lightly and turned, closing the door softly.

Mixed emotions swept through me; it was a full moment before I realized he was gone. I went into the dressing room and found that hot water had been brought up for my use, probably by Dust. I used it after I had stripped off my torn clothes and shoes. I glanced about me furtively now and then at the closed door. I needn't have worried, for it never opened, and when I slipped the soft white chemise over my head and snuffed out the candle, I went to the window and glanced out.

Somewhere in the distance I heard the clatter of hoofs. It came to me then that my bridegroom was riding away, perhaps to his lover already installed at the Three Friars Inn. I fell into the great bed knowing a kind of despair I'd not experienced before, but I was too drained to cry and fell asleep almost at once.

It was Peg who brought me a cup of hot chocolate when I awakened. A fire was crackling on the hearth; it was cozy in the bed, and for a moment I lay in the warmth and softness, feeling luxurious. Then I remembered and sat up guiltily.

"So you're awake at last, my lady," Peg said cheerfully, bringing my blue velvet robe for me to wear. "My, but you slept, and no wonder! Master would not let us wake you. He said you needed the rest." She laughed. "He said you both changed your minds about going away for the honeymoon and decided to come back here. You be so tired out from all the excitement that you slept right through!"

It came to me then that he'd had to invent some explanation; perhaps he hadn't wanted the servants to know I had run away from him and had to go to lengths to cover it up.

I slipped out of bed and put on the robe. "What time is it, Peg?"

"It's past three, but my goodness! How sound you did sleep! I was sure you'd wake up when Jason brought in the trunks, but no. You slept right through all that noise. Master was clear about that, to let you sleep it out." She laughed and went into the dressing room to get my brush.

"I see. Where is he now?" I asked slowly.

"The master? Oh, he has been busy all day, but he did say that when the mistress is awake to tell you he'd like to see you in your grandfather's old study."

This shook me. What was he doing in there? Grandfather's study had been a refuge for me when I was a child. Now the thought of his being there irked me.

When Peg had gone, I went through the dressing room and opened the other door. As I suspected, Heath's presence lingered. Of course, I thought. No wonder he had chosen these rooms. My old one didn't have connecting rooms, and he didn't want the servants to know. So this was to be the way he wanted it.

I dressed carefully in a mauve velvet gown, braided my hair and pulled it into a tight crown on top, then went down to face the man I had married only a day before.

Heath was sitting at my grandfather's old scarred desk when I entered, an array of papers scattered on the surface. He looked up and then stood and came to me. "You do look rested, Honor. I know you must be famished, so I had Mrs. Barrows fix us some tea. We will have it in here." He led me to the chair beside the fireplace where the tea tray was already set. Some of her hot buttered crumpets looked delicious, and I realized I was famished.

Over our tea Heath explained what he had in mind. "I have been going over some plans for renovating the house, Honor. I need your approval, of course, but I thought we could begin at once. How does this strike you?"

"It sounds marvelous," I said slowly, remembering something Father had said of Heath's interest in the Dor and preserving it. I passed him a plate of sandwiches, which he helped himself to, and a generous helping of jam cake.

He smiled at me. "First of all, perhaps we should choose the color scheme correctly for the fabric we shall want to replace. The furniture is good, but the fabric has seen its day. Here are some samples of swatches I had ordered, and I've been looking through them." He went to the desk and brought over the samples.

Soon we were both poring over plans: the painting to be done, new carpets, the mending, and it was all to begin within the week. "I see no reason why it shouldn't begin now," Heath said. "I like this gold velvet, say with a touch of that moss green for the library. How about you?"

I agreed fervently. "I'm sure Grace can help with the needlework, She taught me that art long ago, and I should like to put it to practical use now," I laughed easily.

He gave me a strange, quiet look. "That must be useful to know, Honor. I had thought to bring in—"

I held up my hand. "I wouldn't hear of you hiring someone else for this job. Besides," I smiled. "I do want to see if what Grace taught me *is* worthwhile!"

"Well, that's settled then." We were both sitting near the fire, and he stretched his legs in a lazy fashion, almost content. A burning log snapped. "I wouldn't want to change this room, if you don't mind, Honor. It does have a comfortable atmosphere where one can be oneself, don't you think? The moment I saw it, I told myself, 'I'll use this for my study.' But Mrs. Dare—Grace—informed me that this was your grandfather's study. Do you mind if I use it?"

All the rebellion I had in store left me then. Yesterday might not have happened at all at that moment. Here was the man I knew I loved—had loved from that very first time I saw him; yet a gulf I had not bargained for had come between us. But a new relationship was now taking place, and it was more than I believed we were going to have together.

We had a late intimate dinner in the dining room by candlelight. I found it hard to concentrate on the meal of roast duckling in orange sauce and Chantilly cake for dessert. I was aware of Heath every second, as he was of me.

However, my high hopes were dashed when dinner was over. Heath left the house, and I learned later he had gone to call at the winery. Shortly before midnight I retired to the bedroom and prepared myself for sleep. If I had entertained such hopes that he would come to me this night, I was sadly mistaken, for I did not see him nor hear when he did come back to the house.

I must have dozed off, but it was an uneasy sleep, for I tossed and turned much of the night. Suddenly

I was awake; a man with a masked face was bending
toward me. I screamed then, shrinking back into the
pillow, but the man's long fingers reached for my
throat, shook me, and pressed down on my flesh.

I struggled, but he was strong. I screamed again, but
it only came out as a strange gurgle in my ears. I
couldn't release myself, and he was kneeling on my
bed, his hands pressed into my windpipe.

Suddenly he let go, and I fell back on the pillow.
He ran from the room through the dressing room,
making hardly a sound. I screamed again, and the
door burst open from the hall just as I struggled from
the bed.

Heath stood there, a candle in his hands, and behind him I saw the startled face of Mrs. Barrows, a
ruffled cap on her head and a night robe thrown over
her gown, Dust behind her.

I clutched my throat and tried to speak, but hardly
a sound came out, and I pointed in the direction of
the dressing room. Heath strode across the room and
went through the dressing room and into his own,
Dust following him, while Mrs. Barrows came to look
at me.

Then he came back. "There's no one in there. What
happened, Honor?" His eyes were dark and unreadable. "I heard you scream once, as I was in the study,
so I hurried along up the back stairs and the Barrows
heard me. We came along together."

Still I couldn't speak. "Honor! What happened?" He
took me by the shoulders and stared at me hard.

"Look at her throat, Mister Heath!" Mrs. Barrows
exclaimed, her eyes wide with horror. "She was nearly
choked to death, I'd say!"

Heath looked, and his hands shook as he touched

my neck. "No wonder you can't speak! Mrs. Barrows, get some good hot tea ready, please. And some salve or lotion. And right away. Dust, you get Jason and Tom to search the house and grounds. Whoever did this may very well still be here."

In a short time both Heath and Mrs. Barrows were working with my throat. Heath's fingers were gentle as he massaged it with the rose salve Mrs. Barrows brought up. It was only afterward that I was able to disclose what had happened.

Grace had come in by that time, and she stood by, listening. "But who could want to strangle you, Honor?" she said, horrified. "You've no enemies, have you, love?"

"I don't know, Grace," I managed to whisper. "But he must have heard a sound of someone coming, for he let go and ran through the dressing room. It was horrible!"

A strange look passed between Heath and Grace, but there was no more said. When Dust and Jason reported that there had been no disturbance or a trace of an intruder, Heath said: "Well, we'll discuss it in the morning. The thing for us all to do now is to get back to bed. In another two hours it will be daylight. Come along now."

I didn't argue. The servants left reluctantly, assured that Heath would look after me. I settled down into bed and allowed myself the comfort of knowing I was safe.

Heath did not close the door between our rooms; after all was quiet, the thought came to me that whoever had nearly strangled the life from me would have had to know that Heath was not in that room, wouldn't he? And in advance. Otherwise, he couldn't have escaped so readily without risk of being caught.

Heath said he was down in the study. It was only then I realized that he had been wearing a dark red robe with gold braid on it over his clothes. He had been in his room then. Why had he gone to the study at this ungodly hour?

I couldn't answer that, and I was suddenly chilled by a strange fear.

By morning my throat was very sore and badly bruised. Heath came in fairly early and massaged it again with the lotion as he had done the night before, his fingers gentle on my neck. I wrapped a silk scarf around it and tucked it down into my gown when I dressed and went down to breakfast.

Heath questioned me: "Is there anyone you might have known in London who might have had something against you?" His eyes were wary and thoughtful. "Can you think of someone who might've had it in for you?"

I didn't look at him, for I didn't want him to see what had passed through my mind; there had been that one incident. Had that same person followed me here? It seemed so unlikely, yet . . .

"I've been thinking. Whoever it was must have known you were alone. He must have had no knowledge of your marriage to me. As much as I distrust Anthony Cordell, I must rule him out. He knew we were married. Besides, why would he want to kill you? No, it must be someone else."

I glanced at him quickly. He wouldn't know about Anthony's work with Intelligence, and I could not tell him about my part in it. Not now.

"It occurred to me, Heath, that whoever did this

must have known you were not in your room. How
else could he have escaped so readily? And that means
he had to *know* this house well enough. I feel certain
it couldn't have been Anthony."

He was silent for a while; then he explained that he
was going into Canterbury and would probably come
back with some men to look over the place for a thorough renovating. "These men are supposed to be the
best in preserving antiquities," he said. "You take care
of that throat, and I'll be back sometime before tea."

When he had gone, I had plenty of time to think.
There were spy units everywhere, those for Napoleon
Bonaparte and those for England. I had been fortunate I hadn't been caught at the game before now. But
somewhere I had made that fatal mistake, and now
someone was trying to kill me. I had been followed,
and my life was in danger. Supposing that person
knew about Anthony, too?

All day I felt the servants were eyeing me with odd
looks; their glances were furtive, and the cold, snowy
weather didn't help the gloom that had settled on the
household.

Sometime after noon I told Mrs. Barrows I was going down to pay a visit to Peacock and his wife Nellie.
She suggested I take some of the freshly baked bread
she'd made along with two bottles of medicine I was
taking down. One was for Nellie's stomach ailment,
and the other was some balm for the arthritic Peacock.
My grandfather had prescribed these and had made
them up, showing me the recipe.

Peacock's three-room cottage was covered with ivy.
Today it was close inside, for the chill was great even
though the fire burned brightly on the wide-open
hearth.

Nellie was happy to see me, and her eyes lit up when she saw the bread I brought her. "Bless 'ee, my lady," she said. "Like our Letty used to be, 'ee is, kind and sweet. The good Lord knows how our lives changed since our Letty went as she did." She sighed. I knew the couple had been old when Letty was born to them and that they had been very upset over her recent marriage. But I had heard the story so often that I didn't care to listen again.

I gave her the medicines and told her how to use them. I also told her not to get them mixed up, then asked where Peacock was.

"Oh, he be a puttin' around in the greenhouse, my lady; 'ee might find him there. He do be hurtin' these days with that old ache."

"Well, that medicine should help some. I'll run along now, as I do want to see him about some flowers."

But when I went into the greenhouse a short time later, I didn't see Peacock anywhere. It was a cold day, and I pulled my cloak around me a little tighter. My throat still ached, and that had been one reason I hadn't wanted to linger with Nellie; I was sure she would get around to asking why my voice was so husky.

As I left the place, I thought I'd walk through the orchards to the winery and pay a call on Moll. It was closer this way, and I might intercept Peacock. The gloom of the afternoon intensified, and it was ominously dark as I opened the wicket gate.

My eyes caught a movement up ahead of me on the path that led directly up to the old tower, and I saw the figure of a person in a long gray robe, like that of a monk. Startled, I stepped back a pace into the trees, but I was not seen, for the person never turned around. He walked along swiftly into the gloom and disappeared from my view.

Without hesitation I ran to catch a glimpse of where he was going or had gone, but when I got to the top of the rise, there was no one about. Hesitantly, I went to the foot of the old friars' tower and peered around its square corners, but there was nothing.

It wasn't significant until later when it was brought to mind that the two events—my being attacked and this mysterious cowled figure—had happened virtually on the same day.

When I reached the house, a carriage was drawn up in the courtyard, and Heath hurried toward me to introduce me to the gentlemen he had brought with him. I summoned Dust to have tea brought to the library.

The evening passed without incident, and it was decided the work on the house was to begin immediately.

CHAPTER ELEVEN

I WAS awakened by a light shining in my face. Startled, I almost cried out and sat up in the bed. Heath stood there, gently shaking me.

"Don't be frightened, Honor. It's me," he whispered. He was already dressed in buskskin breeches, and the cavalry pistols were at his side. He began to put on his coat.

"What is it?" I whispered back, puzzled.

"I'm sailing with the morning tide. I didn't want to leave without telling you. Now you mustn't be alarmed. I shall be back within a week, I should think, if all goes well. You are to carry on here as if I'm not gone, that is, to outsiders. The servants know I'll be gone, so there's no bother there." He grinned. "Remember? You're a part of my ship's company, *The Dark Lady*, and I expect you to keep a vigil for me. Agreed?" I watched the smile play around his mouth and in his eyes, and my heart flipped with a strange little quirk.

"Yes, of course."

"I knew I could count on you. Tom will be here in any case, and you aren't to worry. I don't like leaving you. The painters and carpenters will be around the next few days. I've left instructions."

"Will you be back in time for Christmas?" It was less than three weeks away.

"I should think so." He suddenly came to the bed and bent over and kissed me on the lips, warm and hard. "You'll be all right. I shall come back, I promise you that." He turned and with one movement snuffed out the candle and left the room, closing the door softly after him.

My thoughts were in a whirl; of course, Father had said he owned *The Blue Star* and had at one time used it as a merchant ship. So all the servants would know this. But Heath mentioned *The Dark Lady;* surely those outside Tom Pegnally didn't know about that!

Slowly I began to grasp the reason why Heath had gained my confidence: to get my signature on his crew list so that when I became his wife, I couldn't testify against his illegal work or reveal it without condemning myself!

He married me so that he could come and go, either as Heath or Captain Dark, without fear of being caught! How he must be laughing. How secure he must feel knowing his wife could do nothing. If he were caught, then I would hang with him!

Sleep did not come to me the rest of that night, but in the morning I still had not found a solution; I simply involved myself with the task I had set myself to do, that of repairing the cushion seats of the furniture with the material Heath had brought home with him the day before.

Grace and I took pains to match the new with the old, and we set about it with a fervent desire to see it done and moved to other rooms when that one was completed.

Every day new things arrived; I was pleased with the new carpets Heath had chosen; the rich, glowing colors had been matched up beautifully and in complete harmony with the curtains and the chair cushions.

It was then I decided to have my grandfather's bedroom done over to suit Heath's taste. After inspecting the room he had taken, I thought it might please him if we switched rooms. Then I conferred with the painters, and afterward I had my things moved into the other room so that the work could be done.

I used red because I knew that was his favorite color; the wall paint I chose was a cream color, with the curtains and bed hangings dark red with gold tassels.

When it was finished, I placed red roses in an antique vase I found in the attic where Grace and I rummaged through to find adequate pieces of furniture the former occupants thought long outmoded and that fit very nicely into the rooms.

My days were busy, and I found joy in the simple life. Several days after Heath's room was completed, I received a letter postmarked Margate. I thought it was from Father and took it into the library to read. The room had taken on a special air of quiet beauty, and I was pleased with the effect of green and gold.

But the letter was from Anthony, and it read:

"My dear Honor, I must see you right away. It's urgent. I know it must be difficult for you to arrange a time, so I will do so. I'm free on Wednesday afternoon, and I will be in that little fishing village, Friarsgate, any time after one o'clock. Meet me at the waterfront near The Gull. Don't fail me. Anthony."

How provident that Heath was still gone, I thought, then frowned, counting the days in my mind. He should have been back two days ago. It was now three days before Christmas.

Wednesday. That was tomorrow. I could make an excuse to do my Christmas shopping. I had told the servants I wanted to reinstate an old custom my grandfather had started, of having Christmas dinner for the servants in the great hall on Christmas Eve, and they had been joyous about it.

I went in search of Mrs. Barrows to tell her my plans for the next day. While I was shopping, I could meet Anthony and tell him the danger he might be in.

There had been no repetition of that night the intruder had come; my throat had gradually healed, and even the bruises were fading from my neck. It was true the household servants had been on guard, but there had been nothing to be alarmed about since that night.

I found Mrs. Barrows in the kitchen basting a capon roasting on the spit over the fire. At that moment Meg burst in the door, her usually rosy cheeks now white. She was carrying two large flagons of apple wine Moll had sent up. Her eyes were wide with fright.

"He's here!" she shrieked, and I thought she meant Heath had come back. For a moment my heart lurched with a strange thud. "I saw him!" She was trembling and almost hysterical.

"Who's here, for heaven's sake? Have ye gone daft, girl?" Mrs. Barrows looked up at her, her hands on her waist.

"The old mad friar, that's who!" she shrieked again. "I tell 'ee, I saw him with my own eyes!"

Grace was standing in the doorway, and Dust was at the wood box. They both stared at Meg, as a silence pervaded the room.

"Where did you see him, Meg?" I asked, as no one else spoke. Peg came running in, and she, too, was responsive to Meg's terror.

"He was down by that old tower, all in them robes, and he was running like the devil himself was after him!" She slumped down into a chair, trembling visibly.

I stared at their faces; they knew the legend, and although I gave most of them credit as being sensible, down-to-earth Kentish people, I saw this was affecting them deeply.

"Then it's true," whispered Peg, her eyes as wide as her sister's. "He has come back, like they say he would! He's come back to haunt us, and them at the castle, too!"

"I don't believe in them tales myself," declared Mrs. Barrows, bending back over the basting. "But t'is not for me to say since I didn't see him."

"T'is being said so all over the village now, and since my lady was attacked in her own bed, it's worse," Peg murmured. "Ma heard it only yesterday when she went in with Robbie."

"Has he been seen before this day?" I asked, frowning.

"Aye, several times, according to others," Peg said, her hand comforting her sister's with a pat. "There pet, don't shake so."

"Lor', and he was terrible to see! Like a ghost he was, and I near fainted. Never was I so scairt!"

I recalled the person I'd seen not so very many days past, and I couldn't explain that easily; it was uncanny. All the same, I said: "But isn't he supposed to be a ghost? I mean, if it's not an apparition, then surely it stands to reason that someone is dressed up like a friar to scare everyone into believing the old legend. And plenty of people can make themselves believe it."

Mrs. Barrows turned to me, her eyes wide and her face suddenly pale. "But who would want to do that, my lady?" And I knew all too well they were recalling the night of my attacker. It would be too easy to place the blame on a legend, unexplained.

Grace was logical. "Honor is right. Someone must be playing a nasty trick, surely. I don't believe in ghosts, mad friars or not, and neither does Jason. It could be poachers, you know. Jason and I were just talking last night about the poachers stalking the area right now, for times are hard these days."

"And 'ees right," Dust put in. "That's for sure. It be best not to lay more fuel on the fire than's already laid. Not now, it bain't. With the master coming back and all. I dare say he'll not like this talk of mad friars and such!"

As Grace poured some strong cider into a mug and gave it to Meg, I knew what Dust was saying about poachers was true. Sir Mark was one of the most lenient landowners about, but he was also the hardest on poachers. And this winter was hard for those who were destitute.

Mrs. Barrows said to Meg: "No dearie, it won't do to have you wandering around at this time of day, anyway. Take a good long swig of that cider, and let it warm you up some. I might give you girls a piece of advice, and let it be a lesson to you both. Don't go near that old tower. Come up the longer way. Jason will see you, and Peacock's cottage is right on the path. Stay away from the tower and the cove."

An uneasy feeling persisted all evening; it was as if the household had been given a warning, and everyone

was wary of it. Nevertheless, I sent word down to
Tom Pegnally to set his hounds loose that night, and
by morning there was no sign of any prowler on the
premises.

A soft haze had settled over the coast when I took
the gig into the village that morning. Tomorrow was
Christmas Eve, and I wondered if Heath would be
home. I was certain that the servants were more than
anxious to have their new master back, if only for their
Christmas dinner in the great hall.

Father had generously given me a gift of money for
a wedding present, and I happily decided I could use
it for this shopping spree. My spirits were light as I
watched the gulls swoop in from the sea when I entered Friarsgate, and I took the gig to old Mister Bell's
stables.

It had been traditional for Grandfather to give
shawls for the women in his service in the past and a
gift of money to the men, with a basket of food for
every family. I decided to maintain that tradition and
went into a shop where there were some lovely brightly colored shawls on display. I chose the colors I
thought each woman would like and purchased red
and green paper to wrap them in.

I then went into the tobacco store and impulsively
bought a rich coarsely cut brand of tobacco in a pale-
blue glass I thought Heath would like; for Father, a
box of snuff, the brand he used, and a tin of tobacco
for Peacock because I knew he expected it every year.

The next shop was a must, too; I saw a small enam-
eled comb in pale pink set with tiny seed pearls in a
pattern of butterflies on the wide handle, and I was delighted with my find. It was perfect for Cecily.

It was then I noticed a small gold key chain with a medallion in the shape of a sailing ship attached. The proprietor said I could have some initials engraved on it if I wished, and I thought it would be a nice gift for the man I married.

The proprietor smiled patiently at me and said I could come back after two in the afternoon and it would be ready. I left the jewelry shop and sent my packages to Mister Bell's to have them placed in the gig for safekeeping.

Then I went along to the White Hart Inn for a leisurely luncheon to await the hour when I would meet Anthony.

I was seated at a table facing the street with a view of the waterfront and local pub, The Gull, just down the street. I could wait here and when Anthony arrived, I could see him easily.

My thoughts were on what I would tell him; he would have to know I could no longer indulge in spying since my place was now at Friary's Dor. He would also have to know that he might be in danger, even now.

I wondered at the strange enmity between Heath and Anthony; I could not imagine why Heath had been so vehement at my knowing him, but the thought that he might be just a little jealous did send shivers of secret delight through me. I knew I was jealous of Heath's attachment to Marceline Bonet.

In any case there was nothing I could really do now to change things, and I decided to make the most of what was mine. My gaze was on the street while I sipped the hot cider, waiting for the goose patties browned in a wine sauce to be brought for my dinner.

A familiar figure came out of the livery and walked

toward The Gull, a woman at his side, looking up at him. I thought she was laughing, but perhaps she was not. It made no difference, however, for my heart plummeted into the pit of my stomach.

It was Heath and Marceline. They entered The Gull together. If he had wanted to humiliate me, he could not have chosen a more vulnerable time or place to have done it. All my hunger fled, while a strange pain twisted my heart. I knew I could never forgive him for this.

I left the White Hart Inn, my mission forgotten; I was going home. As I started across the street, my name was spoken sharply, and I saw Anthony striding toward me.

"Honor," he said, taking my arm and leading me back into the White Hart with authority. If the waitress was surprised at seeing me again so soon, she gave no sign, and I found myself seated with Anthony in a small alcove with no view of the street.

"You're upset, and I know what has caused it," he said in a low voice. He ordered some strong hot tea, and after it was brought, he began to talk. His eyes mirrored his feelings, and I looked away from him because of the turmoil I felt at that moment.

He reached over and covered my hand with his own. "I asked to meet you because I have a very important assignment, Honor. Where you're living now can be useful, and I find that fortunate."

"I can't help you, Anthony. Don't tell me your assignment because I cannot help you. It's, it's impossible."

"No, it's not impossible. You must help me. I need you."

I shook my head. "I don't want to work for you anymore, Anthony. I must tell you this. I've been found out, and I was followed here. You must be very careful, for it could be traced back to you." I told him of the attempt on my life, of the terror I had experienced.

He was silent in response, and I knew he was in deep thought as we drank our tea. After a while he said: "Heath is known to have had contact with Napoleon Bonaparte's Intelligence in the past month. He has certain information that should have been reported to our Intelligence by now. This he hasn't seen fit to do. I would like to have that information passed on to me. Can you do this?"

I stared at him. "Would you have me spy on my own husband?"

His eyes narrowed, flashing blue green. "Is he your husband in truth, Honor?"

"How dare you ask that!" I cried hotly, indignant, knowing my face was stained with embarrassment.

He smiled, but his eyes never left my face. "Do you think I don't know what's bothering you this very moment?"

"You have no right—"

"I'm making it my right to tell you I know where Heath is right now. I could have told you it would be like this, Honor. It makes my blood boil to see you suffer humiliations like this!"

I put my hands to my face, closing my eyes. "Listen, Honor! I believe Heath is a counterspy for the French and making a huge profit in the process. You mark my words. When this is all over, Honor—" He took one of my hands in his, bringing it to his lips, and kissed it.

"When what is all over?" Heath's voice cut in coldly like a knife. Startled, we both looked up, and I freed my hand guiltily.

No one spoke. An odd fluttering in the pit of my stomach caused me to tremble, and I was glad I was sitting down. Heath was just barely keeping a restraint on his fury. There was a look of murder in his eyes as he looked at Anthony.

"Surely you don't begrudge your wife the company of an old friend, Heath? We were discussing something quite personal when you interrupted—"

"I don't care for your explanations, Cordell!" Heath cut in. "Honor, we must be getting home, and if you have your purchases completed, we'll start. Good day, Captain." His voice was like steel.

Anthony stood up. "Now listen here, Heath—"

Heath took hold my arm, pulling me to my feet. "I said good day, Captain. Come along, Honor."

I could not speak nor did Heath as we left the inn and crossed the street to the livery. He ordered the gig to be brought, had his stallion tied to the vehicle, and helped me into it. He climbed in beside me, and I saw the fury in his face, ready to be unleashed at me.

CHAPTER TWELVE

"HAVE you always met Anthony like this, or is it only when my back is turned?" He kept his voice level, his eyes on the lane in front of us.

When I didn't answer, he said: "I do expect an explanation, Honor. Have you been meeting him in secret?"

"It can't have been so secret there in the White Hart, for all to see, now can it? I did meet Anthony upon invitation. We had some important business to discuss. I saw no reason why I should not have done so." My voice was cool, and I kept my eyes averted. I would not let him see what I felt about his flaunting his mistress about; perhaps even now I was being pitied and humiliated because of it.

"I see. Do you want to tell me about this business you have with him?"

"I do not! I cannot. It is personal." Somehow, I was sick at heart. How on earth did I allow myself to get involved in spying?

"Very well, then, have it your way," he said at last, after a frightening silence. "I should like your cooperation in a matter vital to me—to us. May I ask how and when you had this invitation to meet?" He lifted an eyebrow at me when I stared at him. But his manner was cold and emotionless.

"He sent me a letter yesterday," I said. "I can't see that it makes any difference."

"I'm just wondering how he knew where to write you, that he knew you were at Friary's Dor. To all outside our premises here, you and I were supposed to be on our honeymoon. It seems unlikely that he would have the information unless—" He did not finish, but he left the implication so that there was no mistake what he did think.

"You presume too much," I said angrily. "Servants have a way of talking, you know."

"They are loyal in this, Honor. For all the best reasons you and I have been on our honeymoon to Devon and to Cornwall. Perhaps, then, you mentioned ... ?"

"I did not say anything of the sort," I retorted hotly. "Perhaps Anthony was simply making a guess that we would be back. Anyway, the subject never came up."

We were silent the rest of the journey home, and it was a surprise to find Father waiting for us in the library.

He rose from the chair and took my hand. "I took the liberty of calling today, hoping you might be in, and I find that you have returned already from your honeymoon." He raised his brows slightly as he kissed my cheek.

Before I could answer, Heath said heartily: "The coast of Cornwall and Devon is very pleasant this time of year, Sir Reginald. But welcome to Friary's Dor." He calmly took out his pipe and filled it, then began to smoke, his eyes giving me a warning to say nothing.

"Ah, so that was your destination!" Father laughed, taking a pinch from his snuff box. "Sir Mark and I thought you might take your bride there. He tells me that's your favorite hiding place." He chuckled.

Dust entered with a tray of wine and cake, and Father helped himself to a glass and a thin slice of cake. What he had just said struck home with me; had Heath been there, but with Marceline? Pangs of jealousy tore at me; Heath had once said to me: "You are the first and only woman to sign your name to my ship's company." But might he not have said that for my benefit? Why had he been with *her* today?

"I see that some renovating has already been done, Heath," Father observed, "and I like it. Dust told me you had it done while you were gone, and I must say, it does look improved." His eyes glanced around the room. So Dust had been loyal, I thought.

"Thank you, sir. Honor did most of the choosing and matching colors. We can thank her for it, I believe." He practically willed me to speak.

"There's nothing to thank me for," I said. "I wanted everything to be as it had once been, so it was fairly easy." I glanced down at the cushion I was sitting on and thought of the needlework that had gone into it. Yes, I had achieved some satisfaction.

"Well, it does look the same and yet different—polished, I'd say, instead of the crumbling appearance it always seemed to have." Again Father chuckled as if to himself. "Now, I came with a message from Cecily that she sends her love and some gifts to place at your table Christmas morning," he smiled. "Dust took them. We shan't be coming tomorrow night, for we've been invited to a dinner ball. Mandatory that we appear. However, we shall most likely see you on the day of Christmas at the castle. But then you know about this."

I didn't, but I could see Heath knew, for he nodded slightly in affirmation. When had he sailed in? "Yes. Only this morning Uncle Mark sent us word that we are expected at the castle. I suspect it's a rather formal gathering, too, for us newlyweds. We daren't not show up!" He laughed, mockery in his tone.

"Very good," Father continued. "Now, another pressing reason for my visit today. Honor, I wish you to hear this and take warning. As you both are well aware, illicit smuggling has been the talk of this coast, but there's no need for me to tell you this. Sir Mark has been concerned with it and especially so about one of the most notorious smugglers, a Captain Dark. You must have heard of him, Heath. He has eluded every agent guarding our shores. But now there's talk that he is a traitor to his country, though I can hardly believe the fellow is an Englishman. No true-blooded son of England would openly defy her laws like that."

Silence, strained and taut, fell around us. My eyes were on Heath. But he laughed. "Oh come now, Sir Reginald. There have always been true-blooded Englishmen working for the Crown outside the law as well as inside. Smuggling of this kind can come under the people's protection against the high rate of excise taxes imposed unfairly upon them." He laughed easily. How inane could he be, I thought suddenly, incredulous at the situation.

"But tell me, sir. How do you mean 'traitor'? What has he done?"

Father frowned. "Some strange incidents have been happening, all unaccountable for, and the suspicion is pointed in his direction. I'm certain he's an agent for Bonaparte's Intelligence, or perhaps some members of his crew, for information vital to our safety has been leaking out.

"But here's the situation as it stands: As you may know, I'm in charge of the French prisoners of war in this quarter and those who are kept in the old fortress at the garrison. It's overcrowded, and I daresay, a most miserable existence for anyone. We do the best we can, of course. But they are escaping, confound it, ever since I took command. As many as fifty-five prisoners have escaped, and my guess is that they have been aided in getting back to France. This Captain Dark has been mentioned in regards to providing the ship or ships to smuggle them back to the French coast."

Heath stood up and walked to the fireplace, knocking the ashes from his pipe into the fire. He placed one foot on the rung of the grate, the dark mulberry jacket accentuating the broad shoulders. A trace of laughter was about his mouth. It all might have been a joke. "Is there any proof that this Captain Dark is connected with the escaping French? Has anyone seen him?"

"No one to my knowledge has seen him face to face. He can't even be described with any accurate truth."

"Then, you surprise me, Sir Reginald. Evidence should be the prime motive for suspecting, not hearsay, don't you agree?"

"That's the irony of it. But we've got some men working on it. That's why I'm here, to warn Jason and Tom and all the men on your premises to be alert. There's talk the prisoners are headed this way, or suspected they come this route. To be on the safe side, I'd keep a close lookout." Then he laughed. "When he's caught, as I'm sure he will be, we might learn the truth. He's a rogue, and a tough one. He'll hang from a long rope, and the members of his motley crew will hang with him, you can bet on it!"

After Father's departure with the Christmas gifts I had purchased for him and Cecily, I couldn't help thinking that Heath could, most likely, be that traitor. Hadn't Anthony said he, too, believed Heath to be a counterspy? Father probably knew that Heath was an agent; did he know that Anthony was one? But of course neither of them knew that Heath was indeed Captain Dark.

At dinner that evening I said: "Well, you certainly must have instructed the servants well. Dust lied without batting an eye, it seems."

He grinned at me. "It all boils down to whom they wish loyalty in serving," he said. "You won't have to worry about them."

I looked at him coolly. "Are you a traitor as well as a smuggler, Captain Dark?"

Our eyes met and held for a long time. "What do you believe, Honor?" His voice was low, compelling. In that moment I wanted to believe he was not a traitor. I wanted to believe that he was indeed a true-blooded Englishman helping his countrymen, like Tom Pegnally, fight the excise war.

It was I who lowered my eyes first. "I—I'm not sure what I believe. You must excuse me. I'm rather tired, you see."

"Of course. I'll be up later. And by the way, Honor. Thank you for the room. I like it very much." He walked with me to the door and held it open for me, his smile gentle; then with thoughtful eyes he watched me ascend the stairs.

On Christmas Eve I helped Meg and Peg decorate

the great hall, along with the parlor and library, with the ivy, holly, and box and bay the men had brought in the day before. Heath went out with the men on that morning to bring in the fir tree to be decorated. The biggest logs were carried in for the fireplaces, and the house rang with laughter.

"My life!" cried Grace. "It's going to be like old times, and I for one am glad. I can scarcely wait, for I recall when Doctor Lawrence stood there beside that tree and gave out the presents. We've all missed those good times." She gave me a quick hug and kissed my cheek.

All through Christmas Eve the smell of baking filled the kitchen. Moll Pegnally came up from the winery and helped with Mrs. Barrows and Grace. She was happy, for her Tommy had come home the day before, much to everyone's surprise.

I helped the girls twine the ivy and holly about the pillars in the great hall where tables had been set up for the dinner at precisely five o'clock. We made several Christmas bushes out of wooden hoops and covered them with evergreen and holly leaves, then hung oranges and apples on them to decorate the parlor and library.

By midafternoon, I stood back and surveyed the work of art; it was enchanting, along with the flowers Peacock had arranged in great tubs. There would be dancing afterward, and in my mind's eye I recalled how it had looked those long ago times.

I had been so busy through the day that I hadn't seen much of Heath. Now I decided I should take this time to bathe and dress, for I did not want to be late for this occasion.

I had hot water brought up to my dressing room,

and in a short time I was relaxing in the copper bath, feeling strangely luxurious. My thoughts were idle ones; why had Heath taken so many pains to deceive everyone? That our marriage had not been consummated was a very raw taste in my mouth, but Heath had not wanted that fact known. Why? I was certain that he had been with Marceline, and probably she had been with him all the time. But how could Anthony have known that?

Anthony had known something else, too, and I hadn't liked that. It must show, then, and too clearly, I thought, somehow embarrassed.

I stepped from the tub onto the rug and wrapped a large white towel around me just as the door opened from Heath's room, and I spun about, clutching the towel.

It was Heath. He hadn't bothered to knock. This was his right, and I knew it, but I stepped back. His eyes were upon me, full of question, yet not asking. He wore a red robe with gold braid over the cream breeches. He must have had time to bathe and change, I thought, aware, also, of how his eyes raked over me.

"I thought you might like to fill me in on what part I'm to play tonight," he said anxiously, his eyes not leaving my face. "There are gifts under the tree, and I take it these are to be distributed."

We hadn't discussed it, so he couldn't know. "I believe it will make the servants happy if you do so," I said at last. "My grandfather started the custom, and I wanted to see it reinstated. You don't mind?"

"Oh, not at all. By all means, it does sound original, if anything." He hadn't moved, and I clutched at the towel around me, aware of my wet skin.

I gestured with my free hand. "If you will allow me

some time to dress—" My face reddened.

Still he didn't move, but kept his eyes on me for a long moment. "Of course. You might catch cold with just that towel wrapped around you." He grinned devilishly, and then he closed the door softly behind him.

I dressed hurriedly, choosing a gown I had not yet worn. The creamy satin with its tight bodice and slightly full skirt, was rather daringly low at the neckline. I brushed my hair and braided it into a coronet on top of my head, then slipped into the gown. It was then I saw a small package on my dressing table, a note attached to it.

"I'm sure you forgot this, Mrs. Quiller. I'm sending it along to Friary's Dor. Merry Christmas." It was from the proprietor of the jewelry shop in Friarsgate.

I was debating whether or not I should give it to Heath now when he knocked on the door and entered. "We haven't much time, I'm afraid, if we're to be there at five o'clock." He had changed the robe for the dark red velvet jacket, a white ruffled shirt frock underneath.

"I'll call in Meg to fasten my gown," I said, but he stepped forward and turned me around. "Why bother the maids? I can hook it up for you." His hands were firm and deft, and suddenly he turned me around in his arms. He put one arm around my waist and drew me to him, his free hand went behind my neck and held my head firmly in place as his mouth came down on mine.

His lips were warm and possessive. He kissed me in a slow way that poured flame into my veins. Then he let me go unexpectedly and stepped back, taking a box from his pocket wrapped in red paper and tied with a gold ribbon. "Merry Christmas, Mrs. Quiller," he said in a soft, low voice.

Surprised at his choice of words and the gift, I could only say: "I have a gift for you, too," and gave him the gaily wrapped box. "Merry Christmas."

"I never expected one," he laughed. "But please open yours now. I want you to."

I untied the ribbon and opened the box. Inside was a ruby necklace set with five gems matching the ring I wore. They glowed on the white velvet.

Heath lifted it out. "The Quiller gems," he said. A pair of drop earrings were beside the necklace. "My Aunt Catherine said rubies should be worn at Christmas and by young brides. She says there is something about new brides which cause these gems to glow at their best. Somehow I can believe her."

I was moved almost to tears. My voice was barely audible. "They're simply exquisite, Heath," I said.

"And for an exquisite neck," he said, and suddenly bent down and kissed it. "Here, let me fasten them for you." He put them around me, and I looked into the mirror to fasten the earrings on. The rubies glowed darkly against my skin. I turned to Heath. "I don't know how to thank you."

His eyes seemed to darken, if they could, as they held mine. For a brief moment I went weak with the thought that he was going to take me into his arms again and kiss me, but he did not. He smiled instead.

"I'll think of a way. But let me give it some thought."

I knew my face was scarlet, but I said: "Please open your gift now. I want you to."

Pleasure lighted his face as he took the key chain from the box and held it up. The little ship was indeed an appropriate symbol, and I knew he liked it. He placed it on his jacket, and then we left the room together, almost like two excited children, for the party downstairs.

As we went, I told Heath what was expected of him. "They will be gathered around the tables, and when we come in, they will stand up. We'll take our places—you at the head of the table and I at the foot. We shall eat and afterward distribute the gifts—shawls for the women and money for the men, and of course the baskets of food for each family. Grandfather sometimes let me pass them out as he took them from the tree. You can do as you wish.

"After that you suggest the stirrup cup, the Christmas punch which Moll always makes and is famous for, and the saffron cake is passed around. Then, usually, Peacock will pull out his lute and begin to play, and the master and mistress are supposed to dance the first measures, then leave the hall for them. That's about it."

"That shouldn't be too hard to do. My first duties as the master with his mistress." My heart lurched oddly as he looked into my eyes. "Shall we proceed to the great hall?" He offered his arm just as the clock in the parlor struck five, and we stood before the wide doors, now opened for our entrance.

CHAPTER THIRTEEN

THE servants stood and looked at us expectantly. The tree, which had been decorated in my absense, was now candle-lit, and I exclaimed surprise at its beauty.

As though he had done this every year of his life, Heath took his place at the head of the main table after escorting me to the end, and at his signal we all seated ourselves. The clamor of talk and laughter began at once, with silver clattering amid the platters of roast goose, turkey, sides of beef and mutton, smoked ham and game pies of all size and shape, puddings bulging with sultanas being passed, while everyone exclaimed over the plenty on the table.

Tom Pegnally stood and said: "We all know who is responsible for our plenty here on Friary's Dor this year, don't we, men?" He glanced around the room with his merry brown eyes, and a cheer went up: "Here! Here! Here! We do!"

"His lordship, here, has given us cause to be more than thankful, though we won't mention the very nature of it even among us tonight. We do want to extend our gratitude to him and his new missus by assurring them our loyalty in all things in the coming new year, now that they are newly wed."

Another resounding cheer went up; then Tom sat back down, and everyone fell to their food again while the glasses were filled and refilled with good cider.

At last the dinner ended, the presents were handed out, and the dancing began. Heath and I opened with the first four measures, while the servants encouraged us.

The Christmas dinner was a success. Heath had played his part magnificently as though having done so every year of his life, and when we finally left the hall to the servants, we both had that satisfaction of having given something special.

We stood in the parlor outside the great hall for a moment and Heath said: "I have a suggestion. Why don't we take a short walk down the cliffs?"

"Why not?" I asked, slipping easily into his mood. In a few minutes we had our wraps on and left the house quietly, the merrymaking of Peacock's lute following after us.

It was cold and frosty, but the moonlight was bright, and we didn't speak as we walked along in that clear brilliance side by side. More than once during the evening I had been aware of Heath's eyes as he sought me out, and they had made my heart race.

We walked along the cliffs, the Channel dark with the rough sea. The cove was silent and empty, and it was then I realized the ship was not anchored there.

As if he read my thoughts, Heath said: "*The Dark Lady* is down in Devon under repair, Honor. I came by coach." He turned to face me. "As far as anyone is concerned, we've been on our honeymoon, just as I told your father. It's imperative that we stick together on this. I'm sure I don't have to explain why."

I didn't speak for some time. "I suppose your run was successful by the way Tom Pegnally spoke at dinner."

"Yes. Very."

"Where did you make your run to? Or is that secret?"

He took out his pipe, lit it, and began smoking. The faint glow lit up his face, dark and strong. Then he said: "No, it isn't a secret, not from you. We made our run to France and picked up another cargo for England. That's why I set her to Devon, to deliver the cargo. She'll be sailing into the cove in a day or so."

"Father said you owned a ship called *The Blue Star*."

He saw the perplexity in my face and was amused by it. "She's one and the same. We make legal runs with cargo for the military—amunition, guns, medical supplies, food, and the like."

"But what about the ship's name? Wouldn't she be recognized?"

"We simply paint over her name and she becomes *The Blue Star*, and run up her flag, and she's a respectable brig sloop ready to defend herself when questioned."

I thought of Abdullah on board, and I wondered about the other crew members I didn't see that night. "Who will be sailing her? I mean from Devon."

"Sir Court Gannon, not a member of my crew, but he's in charge of her. At his place there in Devon we have another refuge, you see. You remember Court?" He lifted an eyebrow at me.

"The man who stood with you at the church. Yes, I remember." I waited a moment. "Doesn't your uncle, Sir Mark, suspect?"

He shook his head. "Not at all. And I'm certain we

shan't have any worries that we'll be caught. Everyone will get used to seeing *The Blue Star* anchored in the cove."

"What about the revenue agents? Won't you have to answer to them? Won't they come here?"

"No, not here. We deal with them before we come in. They know us to be mainly war suppliers."

I wanted desperately to ask him about his other mission, but of course I couldn't. That life would probably remain secret, just as mine would.

Heath put his hands on my arms and turned me around to face him. He pulled me close, and his mouth touched mine, gentle at first, then demanding. I yielded to him, lost in the wonder of that kiss, unable to stop it even if I had wished to.

Once he lifted his head, looked at me as if he would never let me go, and his mouth found mine again. We stood there in a mindless wine-dark ecstasy.

Then he whispered: "Honor, you must tell me. What is there between you and Anthony? Has he kissed you like this?" He put his lips on mine again, passionate and demanding, not letting me come up for air, so that I had to beat on his arms to let me go.

"Answer me truthfully now, Honor. What is between you?"

I pulled away from him. "I cannot tell you, I, I'm not free—" He grabbed my arms, holding me to him.

"Not free? Does this mean you are carrying his child and trying to pass it off as mine? Have you gone that far?" His words cut through my heart.

"No," I cried, shocked. "You can't believe that!"

He stared at me. "Then tell me, Honor. Tell me now!" He almost shook me, his grip tightening on my arms until they hurt.

A blinking sense of injustice welled up inside me. How could he dare accuse me of infidelity, while he— I couldn't go on with my thoughts. And never would I tell him I was spying for the British Intelligence.

At that moment a shout from the direction of the house interrupted us: "My lord," Jason called. "Yer wanted at the house. T'is a groom from the castle. He says it's urgent."

Heath turned, releasing his grip on me, but took my arm as we went back to the house. "Thank you, Jason."

The groom was waiting in the parlour, and I went into the library while Heath conferred with him. The scent of bayberry was strong and tantalizing. The yule log was blazing on the hearth cozily, and the sound of the merrymaking in the great hall had not slackened.

A few moments passed before Heath came in and said: "I'm needed at the castle. Some business has come up. I'm not sure how long I'll be gone." His expression was incrutable as he stood close to me.

When I didn't answer, he said: "You can count on this, Honor. I'll be back, and when I do, I shall get an answer from you. Remember that!" He turned and strode from the room. I shivered in spite of myself, for I knew Heath meant what he had said.

I sat down and stared into the flames for a long while, trying to come to some conclusion as to what I should do. But no matter how I tried, I couldn't excuse him for his infidelity to me; for wasn't that his relationship with Marceline—his mistress? And he believed I had been seeing Anthony in *that* way!

My heart was heavy when at last I stood up and took a candle to light my way up the stairs. On impulse I went into Heath's room, taking the gift of tobacco I'd wrapped earlier in the day to place on his dresser where he would see it. Certainly I was in no frame of mind to be generous, but it had been meant for Christmas, and it was best to give it this way.

I placed the candle down on a table and glanced around me; the room had already taken on a definite look of Heath's character; strong and quiet, restful but masculine.

Slowly and methodically I began to go through his personal belongings. There was so much I didn't know about him, and Anthony had asked if I might try and find out. I recalled to mind what Father had once said: "Don't believe all the rumors you hear. And don't begrudge him his past. He's entitled to it as much as you are to yours."

But wasn't Heath begrudging me my past by accusing me of nonexistent relations with Anthony? It certainly wouldn't hurt me to know a little more of the man who meant to know more of me!

The letter was placed on top of a leather-bound copy of *Lyrical Ballads* by Mister Coleridge and Mister Wordsworth, beside his bed on a table. It was a pale fold, the seal was broken, and the handwriting unfamiliar but clear and feminine.

I read it. "Darling, I have been so miserable just knowing you are married to that other woman. I never imagined there would ever be a time I would use that term after what we have had together! But it is a reality now, and I'm facing it. Meeting you in Dover and those three lovely days we had compensates toward mending my broken heart. If I must, I'll take what you offer me if I can be with you. Thank you my darling, for that.

Your Marceline."

I flung the letter down, my face draining of its color. How could he have come through these doors to me, to kiss me as he did and present me with an heirloom of rubies while this letter had been proof of what he'd had with her?

What a fool I'd been! I took the candle and left the room, closing the door after me. Contempt raged within me; at the same time I was torn with jealousy. That he could make my blood race with fire when he touched me only made it worse; he probably made *her* feel that way, too! And that thought filled me with fury.

I paced the floor; I would go to Father, tell him all I knew, and how he used me to gain Friary's Dor. Anthony was right. Heath was nothing but a vain, heartless rogue out to possess what he wanted!

I flung myself down on the bed, burying my face in the pillow, and tried to cry. But tears did not come; I was too angry—too indignant. Although I had known it was true, it took that letter to open my eyes, to see how hopeless it really was and just how much I had deceived myself.

He had gone off—was it to her? And why not? She could offer him what I had not given him. I wanted to die, and I fell back on my pillow more wretched than I had been in my entire life.

I was disturbed from my dreams; I opened my eyes to a cold, dim room, somehow uneasy. I sat up, glancing around the room warily. It was then I saw the envelope on the floor near the door. I slipped out of bed and picked it up, taking it with me to the window where I pulled aside the curtains. Christmas morning, early and cold, had already dawned.

The letter was addressed to me, and the bold, formal handwriting was familiar; I opened it at once. It read: "My dearest. Your life is in far more danger than you guessed. I've been doing some investigating on my own, and my early suspicions are correct. Please do be careful. The man you married is very dangerous. I tell you this because I know it's true. I would ask you not to take this lightly. It could mean your life. Don't try to find out what I asked you to, not now. Just watch your step, Anthony."

A strange tingle of fear rippled along my spine; how had this been delivered, and by whom? Surely Anthony had not been here during the night? My door was locked—I had made a practice of that since that other night. Or had he? I frowned, remembering how Anthony had his way of doing things. But what had he learned about Heath that I didn't already know?

The ship was not here, so he couldn't have known about the smuggling; Heath was too careful to allow that to happen. Then what? I glanced around me, shivering suddenly.

Had Heath come back during the night sometime? I moved cautiously to the dressing room and stared at the inner door that led into his room. I listened; there was no sound. I went to the door and placed my ear against it; then, again hearing nothing, I opened it and glanced about the room.

The bed had not been slept in. I felt I knew the reason for that! I was about to turn and leave when the outer door opened and Heath walked in. My heart skipped several beats before plunging down into my stomach. For a brief moment our eyes met, and I knew I had startled him as much as he had me.

He came in and closed the door, still dressed in the

clothes he had worn the night before. He lifted his brows in an unasked question of my being in his room at this hour.

"You're up early." I heard the weariness in his voice. He took off his coat and flung it down across a chair and walked over to me.

"Yes. I, I thought I heard—" I stopped, aware I was trying to explain my being here, at the same time trying to stop from shaking.

"You're cold," he said, looking at me intently as if to read what he wanted to know. "You'd better get a robe on. I'm sorry I couldn't get home before now. I'm exhausted. Uncle Mark wasn't feeling at all well, but he insists on having that party tonight. We'll have to leave a little earlier than we planned, so I'd better get some sleep." He began to unbutton his shirt.

"I—Yes, of course," I stammered, feeling ridiculous. It occurred to me he was telling the truth. And I could see how tired he was. "I'll go."

"I've given Dust instructions to have me awakened at a decent hour. We're expected to be at the castle at five. Guests of honor, you see." He was close to me now. "Merry Christmas, Mrs. Quiller." And he bent over me and kissed my lips lightly, then stepped back a pace, grinning. I thought he had the look of a satyr at that moment, and I shivered, backing slowly out of that room. When the door closed, I thought I heard him laugh under his breath, and I bit my lips to keep from screaming.

I wished desperately there was a lock on the door, but I suspected it would take more than a lock to keep Heath out if he wanted in.

I could no longer delude myself into thinking that Heath had married me without ulterior motives. Our first meeting had been quite accidental; perhaps the fact I had guessed him to be the captain of *The Dark Lady* had provided him with some amusement, but it had suited his purposes well to make me one of that ship's company because I knew too much.

And now, how much did he know of me? The more I thought of Anthony's letter, the more realistic my fears were becoming. Now I was afraid. The glint I had seen in Heath's eyes a moment ago sent another chill along my spine.

There was today to be faced; I would have to go with him, but I would be careful. He wouldn't dare touch me among so many prominent guests at the castle!

But two strange and unforeseen events took place on the day that followed that altered the course of our lives and of those who lived at Friary's Dor.

It was midmorning when I was rushed to the bedside of Nellie, to find her in convulsions with death but a breath away. I sent for Doctor Simpson, but it was too late. She died within minutes of his coming, and it was quite by accident I learned of what caused her death.

Stricken with compassion, I had left the bedroom and gone into the kitchen, immediately I saw what had happened. A bottle and spoon were on the shelf, and the bottle was open. Then I saw the label on it. Nellie had taken poison instead of her medicine!

No one was prepared for this stunning blow; Nellie had been so gay at the dinner in the great hall the night before. She and Peacock had had a letter from Letty saying she was coming home, and the two of them had been so happy! What a twist of fate. In some way I blamed myself for not seeing to it the bottles were different.

The servants from the house came down to help out; Peacock was brokenhearted, and when at last I left, I, too, was distressed far more than I knew I could be.

Death was always such a final blow, I thought, as I made my way through the garden. Letty was coming home, but it would be only to find her mother gone. Perhaps she could be some comfort to poor old Peacock now.

So deep was I in my distress that I was almost upon him before I was aware; a cowled-robed figure was just ahead of me, careening along the path as if he were drunk. I stepped back in alarm, thinking he had seen me, but he lurched away from me, stumbling farther. I caught my breath sharply. It was a gray-robed figure of a friar!

He was trying to hurry; I was shaken, but there was no time for foolish terror. This was no ghost but a man, and I had to see where he was going and, if possible, who he was! He did not look back; if he had, he would have seen me, but he moved up the path toward the old tower.

Then something else caught my eye; the man was dripping blood. He was wounded, and when he reached the tower, he almost fell against the heavy oak door, pushing it with his weight to open.

I knew I should go fetch Tom Pegnally or Jason, but when I reached the tower, my impulse was much too strong, and I entered cautiously. I was just in time to see the trap door in the ancient floor close. Grandfather had once told me the old friars had used that trap door to go to the secret caves that were under the house and come out at the cove entrance. A convenient, but clever, architectural device. It had been boarded up, however, for the tower had long been declared unsafe. Now here it was, open!

This time I hesitated; no ghost could bleed like this man, but what was he doing here at Friary's Dor, dressed as a monk? I knew then that I had to find out, and I lifted the trap door and started down the dank-smelling stone stairs into a dark tunnel.

CHAPTER FOURTEEN

WHEN the door clanked down above me, I had an uncanny sense of uneasiness. I had thought to be in total
darkness, but the man up ahead had lit a candle,
and once I was down a flight of steps, I found I was in
the tunnel.

As best as I could judge, the tunnel was not very
long; certainly its main purpose had been strictly for a
secret passage of entering the caves in which I knew
Tom Pegnally stored the tuns. I had never been in the
caves, not even when I was a child, for it had been
forbidden.

I took the time to glance around me and above; it
was very good masonry, high enough for a tall man to
walk through without having to bend over, narrow
but not too close, perhaps three arms' length across.
Ever so often I noticed a jutted-out sconce in the wall
for a torch, but there were none now.

The light up ahead wobbled and was suddenly gone,
and I was in darkness. But I realized he must have
turned into one of the cave entrances; I sped along
after him, and sure enough, I saw the light again.

This time I knew I had to be careful or be seen, and
so I crept up to the entrance as quietly as I could
manage. I waited a moment before I entered; I heard

heavy breathing and looked in. The man was tearing off the robe, gasping with pain, and what I saw made *me* gasp, too.

He wore underneath the robe the faded and torn blue uniform of the French army!

All at once the man fell over and hit the floor in a dead faint. I was never more stunned; why was he here, if not a prisoner of war escaping? The truth folded out like a leaf before me. Of course! The cowled robe, the legend that would frighten everyone away, and the cove with its secret caves—a perfect hideaway for the French to await a ship!

But how could it be done unless someone who knew about the legend and the premises well enough was helping them? I knew the answer to that without saying it; my heart thudded inside me. Everything Anthony had said about Heath was true!

I went over to look at the man and started to help him. He was young under that faint beard; his skin was pale, and the loss of blood had probably made him black out. He looked to be no more than eighteen or nineteen, and I saw immediately where his wounds were. They were fresh and bleeding freely.

Suddenly I heard voices and footsteps. I couldn't be caught here like this, so I ran. The cave I was in was a stone room designed to hold huge casks; for the first time I realized my surroundings had been made into a livable space. I moved away from the approaching voices toward the back of this room into another opening. Too late, I saw that it was only a small room stacked high with barrels. I hid behind these as best as I could.

A silence ensued; then I heard Marceline Bonet's voice: "Oh. He is wounded. See? He is bleeding. We'll have to get him onto the ship. He can't stay here like this."

The voice that answered was not the one I expected; I didn't recognize it. "I wonder how he made it this far. Come on. I'll carry him. He's not heavy."

"Well, let's not be gone too long. I want to be here when—"

"Yes, yes. I know. We'll hurry, then." The voice was impatient. I listened to their movements, and it occurred to me that the ship they were talking about was none other than *The Dark Lady*. I wanted to cry, to do anything rather than admit that.

I heard them leave, and the light vanished from the room as their voices and footsteps faded. I crept from the darkness as best as I could and made my way back the way I had come.

When I reached the house and the safety of my room, only then did I realize just how much I had lost.

When I had bathed and dressed, Heath knocked on my door and came in. He looked well rested and had a clean, fresh smell about him. "I heard about Peacock's wife. I'm taking care of the arrangements. I wanted you to know that, and how concerned I am. He's taking her death quite hard." There was something in his voice that was different.

I said nothing. Nellie. That brought me back to reality and what had to be faced. "I feel responsible for what happened to Nellie," I said slowly. "I gave her that medicine, but I warned her then not to mistake it for the other bottle."

"You can't blame yourself for what happened. It was accidental. The doctor has said so, and even Peacock.

But now, it seems, we have something else to face squarely."

I saw the grimness about his mouth, and I almost flinched because of it. "Remember that old legend about the mad friar of Friary's Dor?" His voice was low, intense. I stared at him.

"Well, I can't stop the rumors, but I will have any man flogged if it keeps up! It's ridiculous and getting out of hand. It's now being said that the mad friar is the reason for this death of Nellie's. Servants will believe anything, but I won't have them saying this is why Nellie died!"

"Some of the servants have seen what they believe is a robed monk," I said slowly.

He laughed harshly. "A silly girl's fancy, Honor. We must put a stop to this."

"I agree," I said with meaning. "The person who is playing tricks must be caught to prove there isn't and never was a 'mad friar'."

"Then you do believe that story Tom Pegnally's daughter told?"

"Why not? I have seen someone suspicious like that. I won't deny it." I turned then to the mirror, hunting through a box for the right piece of jewelry to wear with my gown. He said nothing, but I could feel his eyes on me.

"I hoped you would wear the ruby necklace tonight, Honor. My Aunt Catherine would be so pleased to see that you are enjoying it. If I ask you, will you wear them?"

I averted my eyes from his because I was afraid he might read the despair I was feeling. Some men gave their doxy's gems like these rubies—why had not Heath done so? Why had he given them to me? Was this a part of his deceit?

His fingers were warm against my skin as he hooked the necklace. As I looked in the mirror, the rubies glowed against the white of my skin and the gray of the velvet gown.

A short time later the carriage pulled up in front of the house, and Heath and I set out for the castle.

The great iron gates that led to the castle were big and flanked on either side by pillars that were surmounted by two huge armorial lions holding shields. Beyond the gates a wall enclosed a dense park, and as we passed through those gates, a chill of foreboding swept over me.

I had never liked this castle, even from a distance. The castle itself was not large; it was of Norman structure, and the red brick and gray stone mixture showed how much the later centuries had changed the face of the Norman stronghold. The moat was grassy, and I knew that springtime flowers grew there in abundance. Once, years ago, Grandfather had brought me here with him. I had thought the place cold and gloomy.

The guests had not begun to arrive when we pulled up in front of a magnificent doorway, over which brandished a coat of arms. A footman dressed in the Quiller colors of scarlet and gold flung open the heavy nail-studded door, and we entered.

An old man in gleaming livery came forward and bowed low. "My lord, my lady," he said formally. "Please come this way."

"Thank you, Soames," Heath said, taking my pelisse and bonnet, and handing them to the waiting groom along with his own wrap. "Is Sir Mark feeling better?"

"Yes, my lord, I do believe so. However, he is not yet come down. My lord and my lady, Sir Percival and Lady Ernestina are waiting for you both in the drawing room. They asked to have you brought in the moment you arrived."

Heath lifted his eyebrows in surprise. His face seemed to change. "Ah. So the citadel of home and family has been called in for this great moment, to discreetly judge for themselves the quality of the bride the prodigal married!" His laugh was mirthless. "Honor, my dear wife! I must warn you. My father and my mother are snobs of the worst kind. But don't allow them to frighten you. I know how to ignore it." He took my arm, and we crossed the black and white marble hall to the wide curving staircase, following Soames.

When we reached the second floor, I noticed the magnificent ballroom decorated for tonight's event. Across from this was the drawing room to which Soames held the door open for us to enter.

The two people in the room caught my attention at once; I should have known the resemblance was strong between father and son because Anthony pointed out Sir Percival to me at a cotillion we were attending. I doubted that he would recognize me, for we hadn't been introduced.

He was tall and lean, elegantly dressed in a dark green velvet coat cut quite like the one Heath wore. The woman beside him, coolly poised, stared at me through dark brown eyes, and I recalled Heath's warning of their being snobs. I found I could almost believe this as we were introduced.

With a trace of scorn and mockery in every word, Heath said: "How nice of you both to hasten down here to meet my bride, Father and Mother! I dare say you left the 'society' in good hands to make this worth your while. May I present my wife, Honor. And these are my beloved and erstwhile parents, Lady Ernestina and Sir Percival."

I was taken back by Heath's apparent rudeness. But they both seemed to ignore it, accepting it for what it was worth and without question. I curtsied to each of them, and they, in turn, murmured polite greetings.

"Welcome into our family, Honor, my dear," said Lady Ernestina, kissing both my cheeks. She smelled pleasantly of lavender, and the soft tangerine-colored silk muslin and lace suited her fair skin. "Sir Percival and I were both surprised to know we had a new daughter-in-law. But welcome."

"Thank you," I murmured in a barely audible voice, stiffly holding back any comment. How soon would it be before they would turn me aside once Heath . . .

Sir Percival's dark eyes seemed to penetrate mine, but he didn't say much more than "Welcome, Honor" when the door opened and Sir Mark and Lady Catherine came in.

Sir Mark patted my hand fondly in his. "Merry Christmas, my dear. I see you've already met my brother and his wife. Good. Very good." He sighed deeply and sat down, gesturing for the others to do likewise.

I took Lady Catherine's hand and kissed it politely as was the custom. She was a frail little woman, dressed in heliotrope silk, with a diamond broach pinned at the high neckline. She wore diamonds on her wrist and rings on her fingers. I suspected she liked her gems well and wondered that she could part with the ones I wore around my neck and the ring I had on my left hand.

She smiled in her faint vague way and said: "My child, I'm so glad you and Heath are back from your honeymoon so we could have this today. Ernestina and Percival wanted to meet you, and we felt this was one way to accomplish it before my nephew sailed away again."

"It was thoughtful of you to go to all the trouble, Lady Catherine," I said.

"Love is never a trouble, my child. It's a reward we all want to share." She turned to Heath, and it was obvious how she doted on this nephew; Heath was the son she had been denied, and it was there for all to see.

Soames took this moment to announce that the first of the guests were arriving. We were to stand in a receiving line, Heath and I beside his Uncle and Aunt, with Sir Percival and Lady Ernestina flanking the other side. I had mixed emotions as I stood in that line and wondered how it should all come out in the end.

Most of the guests were friends and acquaintances of Sir Mark and Sir Percival—some from London, others from the surrounding homes. Naturally I was the center of interest, for Heath had made quite a reputation for himself as Sir Percival's rebellious son.

As Heath introduced me, I took the outstretched hands and made myself smile at the faces in front of me. Then my father arrived with his party, and I was shocked to see Marceline with them in a daring low-necked gown of exquisite gold silk. Somehow I wasn't prepared for her presence.

When I watched her greeting Heath, I felt a pang of jealousy.

Cecily, gay and enchanting in a silver gown as gossamer as moonlight, embraced me. "Honor! It's so good to see you happy like this. And I must thank you for the little comb. It was dear of you to remember me!" she whispered, and I smiled fondly back at her.

Anthony made up part of Father's party, and when he took my hand, I felt Heath stiffen beside me. Hardly a word passed between us, but I could guess that he wanted to talk with me, and I knew I would have to tell Anthony what I had learned today.

Heath and I opened the ball. In spite of all the fears growing within me, I was secretly proud that he was my companion. He was a good dancer, and I felt light as air in his arms as others followed us on the ballroom floor.

"There are many eyes upon us, Honor," Heath said, his mouth close to my ear. "People are watching us, and I think it might be because they are envious." His arms tightened around me.

"I can't imagine why," I said, a strange catch in my throat.

"I think you can. We are an attractive couple. How fortunate that we should be so! And in spite of everything my parents liked you. You have been accepted in the family."

"They could hardly do otherwise," I said, my voice faint.

"Ah, but you don't know my parents! They may wish me anywhere but here tonight, but for them to be here is the very ultimate. I have it from Mother's own lips that you are a charming young woman and that she means to have us—that is, you, at Stebbens in the very near future! Old Henry and his fat Cassy will simply have to put up with it. Henry, by the way, is my brother, and Cassy is his wife, about ready to have

the heir or heiress, as it may be. You won't like Henry,
I warn you." He smiled, his face suddenly animated.

It seemed strange to hear him talking like this to me
when, in fact, in a very few short hours he would be
smuggling prisoners out of *my* cove!

The dance ended, and there were others to claim
the next set of quadrilles. I did not dance with Heath
again, and though I glimpsed him several times on the
floor, I saw him only once with Marceline.

Then Anthony was at my side and claimed a waltz.
His voice was low as he said: "I've never seen you
look so ravishingly lovely, Honor. I am very jealous
of the man who stole you from me."

I lowered my eyes because what he was saying was
not true; I was not "stolen," but I did know I could
never love anyone else; there would be no one but
Heath, and he wasn't truly mine!

Anthony was watching me; he was not as tall as
Heath, but his eyes were warm, and so was his smile.
He could be comforting to have around, I thought all
at once. Someone I could depend on and who did care.

"Will you have supper with me, Honor?" he said im-
ploringly when the dance was over. The guests were
heading for the dining room where the supper had
been set up. "I'd like that very much," I answered.

No effort had been spared to achieve the bountifully
laden table; down the center ran a streamer of red and
yellow roses, silver and gold-plated bowls held luscious
fruits, and there wre tiny meat pies, fish, fowl and
game pies, and delicacies of all descriptions. A sep-
arate table was set up with drinks, and grooms and
maids were there to serve.

Anthony and I filled our plates, and he led me to a
most unique circular gallery where tables had been set

up for the guests. "This gallery circles the solarium, which is shaped like a rose blossom. Have you been inside it?" He looked at me when I shook my head. "Well. Inside are semicurved stone walls which is a maze of short corridors, all forming the rose petals, where guests can stroll through. I'm surprised you haven't seen it before."

"My first appearance at the castle, I'm afraid," I laughed as I glanced around fascinated. There were rose-colored lamps attached to the wall sconces to give off a soft glow in the gallery. It was a very romantic setting, and whoever had planned it, planned it well, I thought. "It's quite medieval, isn't it?"

"Yes, very much so." We found a table, rather secluded, I thought, and placed our food down. "You sit right here and wait for me. I'll get our drinks and be back in just a minute. Promise me you won't leave."

He reached for my hand and covered it with his own. "I have something I want to discuss with you," I replied.

"Then I'll hurry back." He smiled and left me then.

CHAPTER FIFTEEN

I GLANCED around me in the dim-lit gallery; it was too dim to distinguish other couples and foursomes clearly, but the soft laughter and the music from the ballroom was pleasant. I wondered just where Heath was, and if he were somewhere alone with Marceline.

Her presence had disturbed me more than I cared to admit, but I knew I had to face this fact as it really was; I also knew it was just a matter of time now that I would have to tell my father of what I'd learned this day, and my heart was heavy because of it.

Anthony returned and sat down opposite me. "Well, we can talk at length without fear of Heath interrupting us, Honor," he said grinning. "I saw him leave, and I suspect he might not be back for a while. Now, you did get my note, didn't you?"

"Yes. I'll admit it came as a surprise. But it seems as if you are right. I know that now." My voice was hushed.

He regarded me with a thoughtful gaze. "I'd like to hear what you have to say. Have you learned anything?" He lifted his eyebrows, and I knew what he was talking about.

My heart sank. I began to tell him of the legend, and

he nodded his head several times in acquiescence, his eyes intent on mine all the time. Then I told him of how Father had told Heath and me of the prisoners of war escaping from the fort.

"They are coming to Friary's Dor, dressed as cowled monks, just like the legend, to wait for a ship in the cove," I said in a low voice.

He stared at me. "How do you know this?"

"I followed one. He went through the orchard and up to the old tower, and I followed him there. It was really simple; the tower has a trap door that leads down to a tunnel to the secret caves by the cove." I told him of this morning's experience.

He put down his fork and stared. "But that's the answer! It would be the logical way, wouldn't it? To use the legend like that to frighten the servants so they wouldn't be inquisitive. My God, Honor!" He sounded incredulous. "You've discovered the answer! Did you see the ship?"

"No," I said heavily. "But Anthony. I know Marceline Bonet was there. She came in with someone, and they took the wounded soldier to the boat."

"They? Who—" He lifted his eyebrows, and his face darkened.

"It was someone I didn't recognize," I said hurriedly.

"Sweetheart," he said suddenly, his voice soft with tenderness. "You must have known about Heath and Marceline? You know he has a brig called *The Blue Star*. It stands to reason that he is behind all this. Marceline Bonet is a French spy; I know this for a fact, and I've been watching her for—well, I won't go into that now. And if she was down there, you can be assured Heath is behind it all." His face was grim.

"Do you know if *The Blue Star* was in the cove this morning?"

I felt a chill along my spine. He knew nothing about *The Dark Lady* so far; he would have mentioned it if he had. Unexpectedly, he reached over with one hand and covered my own where it lay beside the plate.

"Honor, if *The Blue Star* is in the cove, that means she will sail tonight. You know this, don't you?" His smile was disarming, touching because of his concern now. "And if my guess is right, he has already left here to see about it. This is disturbing news. If I could manage to get there before he sails—he can't go out without the tide, not from the cove. . . ." He stopped, a sudden light of decision in his face.

"Can you go with me, Honor?" he said softly. "We can leave without being seen. I would like very much to have you show me the tower and the tunnel. Perhaps we can even get back here before you're missed; Heath is gone; perhaps even Marceline is gone! I must make sure, and I must have evidence. It comes to that."

I didn't have to consider; I wanted to go, even if it meant my having to come face to face with Heath and Marceline. In the end I would have to, so. Why not get it over with?

"Very well. I will go with you, Anthony."

He pressed my hand. "You must trust me, sweetheart. You won't regret this, I promise you."

We had no trouble leaving the castle. Anthony drove the carriage without any fear of accident. He was excited, and I caught the mood, but I somehow wished I had told my father.

When I voiced this to Anthony, he said: "He will

know in plenty of time, Honor. But you must know this is going to implicate your father's wife. I know she is Marceline's contact—"

"Not Father!" I cried. "He is no traitor!"

"Of course not, sweetheart," he said softly. "Not Sir Reginald. Just his wife. He didn't—he doesn't know."

Poor Father, I thought sadly. I was growing fond of Cecily, too. But of course what Anthony said was true enough. It all fitted like pieces of a jigsaw puzzle. I wanted to cry.

We left the carriage a distance from the house and went on foot down the cliffs and walked along there to the tower. I told Anthony of Tom Pegnally's hounds, and we decided not to set up any warning.

Just as I had done earlier, we entered the tower and trap door, and let ourselves down into the tunnel by way of the stone stairs. This time I had thought to bring a candle, but Anthony suggested that we not use it if at all possible. So it was dark, and we had to feel our way at times after adjusting our eyes to the pitch black.

It was when we reached one of the caves that Anthony gripped my arm and pulled me to him. "My God, Honor!" he whispered in my ear. "It just came to me, and by God I think I'm right!" He was excited, a tremor in his voice.

We stood staring around us, and I looked at him. He said: "Heath could be, and most likely is dealing in smuggling! Look at all this contraband! Why, we're right in the middle of a smuggling den!"

Something like a groan escaped my lips, and Anthony took the candle and lit it, the cave was suddenly illuminated around us. He inspected the contents of the room, the proof of his sudden perception. He turned to me again.

"What do you know about this, Honor?" He gripped my arm tightly. "You do know something, don't you? You must tell me what it is."

I could only stare, my heart beating furiously.

He was searching my face intently. "Honor, I must know what it is. Don't you see, if he is a counterspy, then your life here is doubly in danger, and he is simply using you—his marriage to you—to make this his *lair!* He might even be connected with that notorious Captain Dark. Is this what you know?"

My voice was husky with emotion as I said: "Heath is that captain, Anthony—" I could hardly get the words out.

Anthony stood quite still, his eyes wide and very blue upon my face. "What are you telling me, Honor?" he demanded, though his voice was soft. I couldn't answer, but the sudden movement in the doorway beyond him caused my heart to stampede oddly. I felt cold and sick.

In the entrance, framed by the blackness of the tunnel behind him, stood Heath, his eyes narrowed and hard. My hand went to my throat, and Anthony saw my expression.

He whirled about, his hands whipping a pistol from his belt, cocking it simultaneously. In that split second two charges exploded, rocketing across that small space with an ear-splitting roar.

Unreality swam dizzily about me as waves of sickening coldness swept over me. I fought off that unreality; Anthony's body lay at my feet, but I could not scream.

Heath stood just within the entrance, his eyes on my

face, and I heard running footsteps. Then Heath began to move toward me, and I heard voices. A strange darkness began to wash up from that cave, and I was falling. . . .

From a long way off a voice spoke in that blackness. "Grab her! We'll take her to the ship . . ."

I put out my hands in a futile gesture, but a dark shadow towered over me, and a crimson turban gleaming above a black satin face then stooped toward me. . . .

I sank into merciful oblivion.

I was dimly conscious of a rocking motion beneath me, and I opened my eyes. My stomach churned, and I rose from the bed I was lying on and found a basin just in time. After a long wretching I was weak; I stumbled back to the bed and fell upon it. A lantern hung directly above me, swaying to and fro.

When I opened my eyes again, the rocking motion had ceased. I glanced around the room, which was vaguely familiar, and I allowed myself a moment's reflection. Sunlight was dancing through a window in the back, and a round porthole was open to a vivid sky. I sat up, shocked, memory flooding back. I was in the cabin of *The Dark Lady!*

I saw a ewer of steaming water, and a towel had been placed at my convenience; someone had been in here. It was only then I was aware that I had nothing on beneath the blanket. My clothes were nowhere in sight.

The blood rushed to my head, and I fell back weakly. I remembered everything except how I got in here. I felt grimy and had a sour taste in my mouth. I waited a few moments, and since I heard nothing, I crept from the bunk and stood on the floor to wash my body. It was then I noticed a scarlet embroidered silk robe hanging from a peg at the foot of the bunk, and I wrapped this around me tightly.

My hair was unbound and untidy; I searched the shelf above me and found a comb, then went to the window to look out. The harbor, which I didn't recognize, was large. The water was gleaming in the afternoon sun, and another ship, all scarlet and gold, was close by. Sounds of the afternoon were muted, almost sleepily so, and the tantalizing smell of food cooking somewhere filled the air.

I combed my hair while I tried to reason just why I had been brought aboard *The Dark Lady*. Certainly the memory of Anthony lying at my feet was not just a nightmare but a reality I should never forget. Why, then, hadn't Heath pointed that gun at me, too? Was it a scheme of his to kidnap me and make it look as if I had plotted Anthony's death along with him?

I saw it all flash before me again: that moment of horror when Anthony turned and met Heath, the blinding explosion, and that hard, cold look on Heath's face as he walked toward me. . . .

CHAPTER SIXTEEN

THE sound on the deck outside brought back sharply the reality I was to face now. A sick, bitter anger tightened my throat; I knew I was frightened of Heath now, but I was going to try to not let him see it. I braced myself and stood where I was, hugging the red robe to me, my feet bare on the polished floor.

"So you've come around at last," Heath said, coming in and glancing at me, a tray in his hands. His voice was curious, pleasant, and I saw none of the hardness I remembered in his face.

He placed the tray down on the table and came over to the window where I stood. I stepped back a pace, scornfully watching him. He looked at home in the white shirt open at the throat, the dark hair on his chest showing beneath.

"You're not sick now?"

I shook my head after a moment, and he smiled gently. "You were, you know, at first. Very sick, indeed. And that makes you a very poor sailor!" He laughed, and I wondered what there was to laugh at.

"And I can guess that you're hungry now. Abdullah did his best at roasting a swan for us. I thought we might have dinner together. Do you feel up to it?"

I stood where I was, not speaking; how could he expect me to act as if nothing had happened? I said through stiff lips: "You killed him, didn't you?" I kept my voice level, but my heart thudded oddly, and a tremor ran through me.

His eyes were thoughtful for a moment before he spoke. "Yes. I killed him, Honor." He went over to the table. "I can see there are explanations you will need. But first, let us have some food. I see you found the robe. Your clothes weren't suitable after you'd been sick." His eyes went over me, and to my dismay I reddened.

He took two plates and knives from the bulkhead locker and a clean cloth, arranging them on the table, then fetched a bottle of wine and some glasses, placing them on the table, too. He pulled the chair out for me, and reluctantly I went over and sat down, knowing there was nothing else I could do. I was drained of all emotion.

I watched as he uncorked the wine, poured it into the glasses, and sat down across from me. We both began to eat. The roast swan was the tastiest I had ever eaten in my life; I was famished. As he held the roast leg in his hand, I followed suit. We wiped our hands on the cloth and drank the sweet cold wine in the golden hush of the warm afternoon.

Idly, I wondered where we were anchored, it was so pleasant and warm, and then it occurred to me that wherever we were now, it was not Friary's Dor, that perhaps I had truly lost it forever. Tears filled my eyes, and I had to blink them away.

"Did he mean that much to you, my darling?" An odd light was in Heath's eyes and in the tone he used.

I knew what he meant, but I could not answer; I shrugged my shoulders instead.

He stood up, went over to the porthole, and stared out, his hands in his pockets. His voice was soft when he spoke. "You didn't know Anthony was the traitor, did you?"

I was not prepared for this. "Anthony was no traitor —no! I can't believe that."

"You mean you won't believe it, is that it?" He turned to face me, his eyes haunted. "But it's true. Marceline confessed—"

"Marceline!" I cut in. "She is a French spy—your lover, mistress—whatever you choose to call her!" I choked, and I was suddenly shocked by the flood of emotion that poured through me.

He came over to me and took my hands in his, pulling me to my feet. "You were jealous of her?" he asked simply. "She was not my mistress, though she would have been had she had her way. I told you once I didn't care for gold hair and green eyes. Remember? "

I pulled my hands free from his because I didn't trust myself. "I read that letter. You can't change that fact!" I couldn't look at him.

He was silent for a moment. Then he said quietly: "I have a letter for you written by your father. In a little while I want you to read it. But for now, will you allow me to explain?"

I kept my back to him, staring out the stern of the ship at the blue water dancing in the golden light.

"I learned about your working for our Intelligence Unit, Honor. My father told me. Anthony put you up to it. He knew a good thing when he saw it." His voice was grim, but I realized all at once, and with a rush of horror, that Heath had had his revenge. He had killed the man he so hated from childhood.

"Then you should know Anthony could not, would

not be the traitor you have accused him of being! He was not like that." Again, a bitter anger swelled in my throat, and I could not go on.

He seemed to ignore my defense of Anthony's character and continued. "Anthony was a counterspy—oh, yes. He was working for the French as well as for the British! That is how he knew Marceline so well.

"It all started when Anthony learned from my father, and through devious methods, I might add, that I was being sought to marry Sir Reginald's daughter. That made him furious, for I truly think he had you lined up for his own." His eyes flashed at me and I winced inwardly.

"That brought back all the old enmity; you see, Anthony resented my being Percival's son. Why? I only understand that he felt cheated by his birth, and why it should have been me is only because we both were thrown into each other's lives in childhood. No one's fault really except the customs of our society and times." He reached for his tobacco tin and his pipe, and for a while he didn't speak.

I watched him as he stood gazing out the window. At length, he said: "I was taken by surprise when I saw him at your father's house in Margate, the night we were married, Honor. I had no idea that he could know you. I was near wild with jealousy. And that he had suddenly become attached to your father's staff as aide-de-camp was baffling. I didn't know then, of course, what I know now—that he was a counterspy."

"What proof—" I didn't recognize my voice.

"He was working very hard to get something he could use against me, and Marceline Bonet was one way. I met Marceline less than a year ago, and from the start she had designs on me. 'The wrath of a woman

scorned in love,' is always a good motive, I suppose.
But she worked with Anthony; it was Anthony who
followed you that night in St. Johns Wood; yes, I took
the trouble to find out, and it was Anthony who came
into your room that night and tried to frighten you
into believing it was I who tried to strangle you. He
succeeded in making you believe I was going to kill
you."

I stared at him, my eyes wide. "But why on earth
did he want to do that?" My voice was faint.

"He wanted you for himself. And you were leaving
with him, weren't you?"

"Is that what you thought?"

"What else could I think? You left the castle with
him. Soames saw you leave together."

"Anthony said you might leave with the tide. He
wanted to see the caves—" I was suddenly nervous. "I
knew about the French prisoners escaping."

His look was calculated. "How did you find out?"

I told him.

"So you told Anthony? At the castle?"

I nodded. "He saw you leave. We thought—I
thought you were helping to smuggle them over to
France. I recalled you said the ship would be in the
cove—" I faltered.

"There was a ship there, Honor, and you were going
to be on it with Anthony. Marceline confessed that
she had been helping Anthony plot your abduction;
that way she would have free rein to pursue what she
wanted."

"But the letter—?"

"She wrote the letter, and Anthony placed it where
he knew you would see it. It was a diabolical plan of
both; but what they didn't know was the identity of

Captain Dark. It seemed convenient and very plausible to place the 'traitor label' around his neck when all the while Anthony wanted it around mine."

My head was swirling with unasked, unanswered questions; how could I explain that I revealed his identity to his enemy? I should not, I knew. Instead I asked:

"How did you know where to find me?"

"Tom Pegnally came to the castle with word that a strange ship was in the cove; naturally, we were expecting *The Blue Star*. I left, and that was when I caught Marceline. I had to force her to tell, and I don't mind telling you it took some doing. But she admitted all of it. *The Blue Star* sailed in and took the French ship."

I sighed deeply. "Poor Cecily! What will become of her? Father loves her so very much." I was half-talking to myself.

"Marceline was blackmailing Cecily, Honor. She confessed it; I believe it's all in the letter from your father."

We were both silent, each in our thoughts. It brought back the warmth of the afternoon outside the ship. "Where are we? Why did you have me brought aboard?"

Warm lights shot up in his dark eyes. "We're in Mount's Bay, on the Cornish coast, Honor. All that was five days ago. This is New Year's day."

"You abducted me. There's so much I don't understand—"

"There will be time for all that. But for now, will you tell me something?" We faced each other, the window between us.

"What do you want to know?"

"What did Anthony mean to you?"

"He meant nothing to me, Heath," I said honestly, as foolish thoughts whirled around my head.

He came to me then, his arms going about me, holding me close. I lifted my head, and he kissed me gently, then more deeply. "Honor—Honor," he whispered. "Do you love me a little? Even if you do not, stay with me. Could we not take this time and start our lives fresh? You must not ever be frightened of me!"

His eyes glowed at that moment as I said: "I shan't be frightened of you—not like this. But I thought you loved *her*."

"Never!" he said in a deep tone that touched my heart. "I loved you from the start. Remember how I kissed you that first time? I believed you loved me, too. But when you ran away from me on our wedding night, I was near wild with jealousy. I thought you must be in love with Anthony! I wanted to be the first one to make love to you. When I found you, I was so relieved, yet so blind with anger that I wanted to hurt you. Then I saw that look of fear on your face, and I couldn't—I simply couldn't!" He kissed me. "I meant to win your heart—to go slowly and gently, and you would come to me—"

He pressed his cheek to my hair. "I love you, Honor."

"I love you, too, Heath—I have from the beginning. You should know that."

He picked me up in his arms and carried me to the spacious bunk. We did not speak; there was no need to. He was gentle, he was tender, and all those things only a lover can be.

Our honeymoon along the Cornish coast lasted for

four weeks; it was a time of discovery of one another.

When we returned to Friary's Dor, it was to take up the reins of a long and satisfying, yet sometimes turbulent life. Heath continued in his secret role as *Captain Dark* and his life of smuggling when the cause warranted it; I never had to reveal to him that I had betrayed his secret once, for that betrayal had gone to the grave with Anthony Cordell.

Father and Cecily retired to Gardenscroft to await the birth of their first child, a son, the following year. When Cecily had confessed her youthful indiscretion to Father, she was forgiven for her part in the odious crime. It was through Cecily that I learned of Marceline's death after she had been exiled from England shortly after Heath and I returned to Friary's Dor. She was drowned while crossing the Channel during a winter gale.

Old legends do not die easily, but there were no incidents to blame on the legend of the "mad friar." It is still told, but those at Friary's Dor know the truth.

When Sir Mark died the following year, Heath and I did not move to the castle; we planned that our heirs should have it, and we lived our own life at Friary's Dor, content within its walls.

GOTHIC MYSTERIES
of Romance
and Suspense...

Dell Books 75¢

If you cannot obtain copies of this title from your local bookseller, just send the price (plus 15c per copy for handling and postage) to Dell Books, Post Office Box 1000, Pinebrook, N. J. 07058.

HOW MANY OF THESE DELL BESTSELLERS HAVE YOU READ?

1. **BRIAN PICCOLO: A SHORT SEASON**
   by Jeannie Morris $1.25
2. **THE GIFT HORSE** by Hildegarde Knef $1.50
3. **MADAME** by Patrick O'Higgins $1.50
4. **THE HAPPY HOOKER** by Xaveria Hollander $1.50
5. **THE TENTH MONTH** by Laura Z. Hobson $1.25
6. **ON INSTRUCTIONS OF MY GOVERNMENT**
   by Pierre Salinger $1.50
7. **THE SCARLATTI INHERITANCE** by Robert Ludlum $1.50
8. **THE PROFESSOR** by Jack Lynn $1.25
9. **FIELDS FOR PRESIDENT** by W. C. Fields $1.25
10. **THE DOCTOR'S QUICK WEIGHT LOSS DIET**
    by Irwin Maxwell Stillman, M.D. and
    Samm Sinclair Baker $1.25
11. **THE MAFIA IS NOT AN EQUAL OPPORTUNITY**
    EMPLOYER by Nicholas Gage $1.25
12. **THE ONE-EYED KING** by Edwin Fadiman, Jr. $1.50
13. **POTATOES ARE CHEAPER** by Max Schulman $1.25
14. **THE ONION EATERS** by J. P. Donleavy $1.25
15. **AMERICA, INC.**
    by Morton Mintz and Jerry S. Cohen $1.50

If you cannot obtain copies of these titles from your local bookseller, just send the price (plus 15c per copy for handling and postage) to Dell Books, Post Office Box 1000, Pinebrook, N. J. 07058.

"Extraordinary is the word to be used first, last, and repeatedly about this book . . . . Anyone who meets Karen, even on paper, will postpone resigning from the human race."

—*The Saturday Review*

KAREN 75c
Marie Killilea

As told by her mother, the inspirational story of Karen, who—despite a handicap—learns to talk, to walk, to read, to write. Winner of the Golden Book Award and two Christopher Awards.

WITH LOVE FROM KAREN 75c
Marie Killilea

Written in response to thousands of letters, this sequel to *Karen* tells of her growth from seven years old into womanhood and relates more about the open friendliness and spiritual plenty of her family.